A King Production presents...

Still The Baddest Bitch

JOY DEJA KING

This novel is a work of fiction. Any references to real people, events, establishments, or locales are intended only to give the fiction a sense of reality and authenticity. Other names, characters, and incidents occurring in the work are either the product of the author's imagination, or are used fictitiously, as those fictionalized events and incidents that involve real persons. Any character that happens to share the name of a person who is an acquaintance of the author, past or present, is purely coincidental and in no way intended to be an actual account involving that person.

ISBN 13: 978-0986004544
ISBN 10: 0986004545
Cover concept by Joy Deja King
Cover layout and graphic design by www.mariondesigns.com
Typesetting: Keith Saunders

Library of Congress Cataloging-in-Publication Data;
A King Production, King, Deja Joy
Still The Baddest Bitch: a series/by Joy Deja King
For complete Library of Congress Copyright info visit;
www.joydejaking.com Twitter: @joydejaking

A King Production
P.O. Box 912, Collierville, TN 38027

This Book is Dedicated To My:

Family, Readers and Supporters.
I LOVE you guys so much. Please believe that!!

"Flyer Than A Piece Of Paper Bearin' My Name/ Got The Hottest Chick In The Game Wearin' My Chain..."

Jay Z—Public Service Announcement Interlude

A KING PRODUCTION

Still The Baddest Bitch

A Novel

JOY DEJA KING

Aaliyah

"Mommy...Mommy...wake up! Pleaaaase, Mommy, wake up! You can't die. Dear god, I beg you, please, don't let my mother die!" During the ride in the ambulance, those words I pleaded to god, as I watched my dad hold my mother's lifeless body in his arms, kept replaying in my head. I seemed to be trapped in somebody else's nightmare, but the more I witnessed the paramedic and emergency medical technician doing everything they could to keep my mother alive, I had to accept this nightmare was my reality.

"Daddy, she can't die...not like this," my voice trailed off as I held on to my father's hand tightly, hoping it would somehow bring me strength.

"I've done this before. When does it stop? I

guess never." When my father said those words, it took a minute for them to sink in.

"What do you mean you've done this before?"

"Your mother almost died in my arms years ago. Before you were born. She was shot, just like she was today, and lost our baby. That was the worst day of my life and now this is the second."

This was the first time I heard anything about this. Before I could ask my father to further elaborate, we had arrived at the hospital. In an instant, the pace went into overdrive. They rushed my mother into surgery and all we could do was pray. I grabbed onto my dad's arm and held it tightly.

"Please, move aside," a male voice barked at us as.

"Omigoodness, that's Genesis," and then I noticed my dad. "Daddy!" I yelled out when I saw them being brought in on stretchers. Right behind them was Amir. "Amir, what happened? Is it bad?"

I was so caught up with what happened to my mother, I had no idea Genesis and my dad had also been hurt. I prayed they weren't on the brink of death, like my mother. This nightmare was getting worse and worse with each second.

"They've both been shot, but the injuries

aren't life threatening. It's not bad."

"Thank goodness. There's only so much more of this I can take."

"How's your mom?"

"Not good," I said, putting my head down, now wanting the tears to start pouring all over again.

"Aaliyah, I'm sorry," Amir said, holding me closely.

"I don't know what I'll do if she doesn't make it."

"I got here as soon as I heard. How's Precious?" I looked up and saw Lorenzo standing in front of us. Instead of answering Lorenzo's question, I continued to cry.

"It's not looking good," Amir said, answering for me.

"No, not Precious," Lorenzo kept repeating, with his voice breaking up. He put his hands up and repeatedly shook his head, as if in denial. He then walked off and I saw him talking to a triage nurse. I guess Lorenzo was searching for the same answers we all wanted.

Amir and I went to sit down next to my dad. We all remained silent, as if scared to speak. This went on for what felt like forever and the silence made me feel like my head was going to explode.

"Aaliyah, do you want anything? I'ma go get something to drink."

"I'll take anything with caffeine, since I'll be up all night."

"What about you, Supreme. Can I get you something?"

"I'm dad."

"Dad, you sure you don't want anything?"

"Yes," he said, and walked off. I knew my mother's condition was eating him up; hell, I was barely keeping it together, but I hated seeing him so broken up. So many thoughts were going through my head and as I began to get lost in them, from a distance I noticed Lorenzo. I decided to go speak to him and see if the triage nurse had told him anything we didn't already know. I seriously doubted it, but I was grasping for any sign of optimism at this point.

As I got closer, I realized Lorenzo was on the phone. He was in a deep conversation. I decided to get close enough where I could hear what he was saying, but he didn't notice me.

"Dior, I can't come to L.A. right now. Someone very close to me is in the hospital. Yes, it's a woman.

Why are you asking me that?"

Damn, I wish I could hear what this Dior chick is saying, I thought to myself.

"Yes, I love her." There was a long pause before Lorenzo continued, "and I do love you, too," he said, in an almost frustrated tone. "I don't want to get into a discussion about my feelings for you or Precious, right now. I have to go. I'll talk to you tomorrow."

When Lorenzo got off the phone he turned around and I could see the surprise on his face when he saw me. "Aaliyah, I didn't realize you were standing over here."

"I'm sure you didn't, being that you were so deep into your conversation," I said sarcastically.

"I'm assuming you were listening."

"Of course I was. You claim to care so much about my mother, but you were on the phone with some chick named Dior. You are such the quintessential player."

"It's not like that, Aaliyah."

"So says the man that's on the phone proclaiming his love to another woman, while my mother is fighting for her life."

"Your mother knows all about Dior. She was a

woman I was engaged to before I ever met Precious. I thought she was dead. During my relationship with your mother, I found out Dior was alive. That's why Precious broke things off with me, but I never stopped loving her. Honestly, when I heard that she might die, I realized how in love with her I am. I want to be right by your mother's side when she wakes up."

"So, you think she's gonna make it?"

"I have to believe that and so do you. I can't consider anything else. Aaliyah, I know you never really cared for me."

"It's not that. It's just that..."

"You blamed me for breaking up your mother and father," Lorenzo said, finishing my thought.

"I did blame you initially, but like I told you before, I realized their marriage was already over before you came into her life. I will admit, I always wanted them back together and felt you were in the way."

"I get that. Please know your mother is very important to me. After Dior, I didn't believe I could ever fall in love with another woman again. Precious proved me wrong."

"She has that affect on men," I smiled. "I do believe you love her, Lorenzo, and I'm glad you're here. My mother needs everyone's support right now, including yours."

I glanced over at my dad and then back at Lorenzo. Both men loved her and so many other people did, too, but none more than me. If my mother didn't survive, all of our lives would change and nothing would ever be the same again.

Precious

"Clear the area! Prepare this patient for emergency surgery!" that was the last thing I heard, before I completely lost all consciousness and went to another place. This brought back so many memories, but this time was different.

Not this again. Dear God, I was here once before. Fighting for my life and the life of my unborn child. I survived, but my baby didn't. The child I shared with Supreme was taken away from me, without even having a chance to hold our baby. I want to live, but I feel so weak.

It's not like when I got shot the first time. Back then, deep down inside I could feel I was alive and would survive. This time I felt death lingering over me. I wanted to go back to my family and be with my children, but voices and noises were sounding further and further away, 'til I heard nothing at all. My vision had faded to black, but it wasn't scary: there was this peaceful calmness that had come over me.

"My baby, are you sure you're ready to join me?"

"Mother, is that you?"

"Of course it's me. I've been waiting to be with you again, but I didn't think it would be so soon."

"Am I dead?"

"I can't answer that question, but I can show you the way."

Years Earlier...

"Happy Birthday to you, happy birthday to you, happy birthday to Precious, happy birthday to you! Now, blow out the candles!"

I took a deep breath and blew as hard as I could, until I had blown out all seven candles.

"Yeah," my mom clapped. "Here, open your present."

"Mommy, what did you get me?"

"You have to open it and see."

I ripped open the Hello Kitty wrapping paper. Inside was the beautiful black doll I had seen a few weeks ago, when my mom and I were walking down the Ave.

"I can't believe you got this for me! I love you so much, Mommy!"

"I love you, too, baby," she said, holding me tightly. "Now, let's eat some cake and ice cream."

Knock...knock...knock

"You get the bowls and I'll get the door, okay baby?"

"Okay, Mommy."

"Nathan, what are you doing here?"

"I came to see my favorite girl."

"I'm busy. I told you before that today is my daughter's birthday. Now, please leave."

"Hey there, pretty girl. Uncle Nathan brought you something for your birthday," the man said, handing me a present.

"I don't want it," I said, rolling my eyes at the

man. I didn't like him. Every time he came around my mother, she acted different and in a bad way, not good.

"That's no way to talk to your Uncle Nathan, is it," he said, rubbing my head like I was his pet dog or something.

"Nathan, I have to go. We're about to cut the birthday cake." As my mother was shutting the door, Nathan put his foot in the entrance to keep it from closing. He then pushed it back open.

"I ain't going nowhere. I need you back to work."

"I told you I'm done wit' that. I'm cleaning up my life. Being a better mother for my child. Now, leave!"

"Ho, I own you. You don't tell me when to leave. Now get dressed, you going to fuckin' work!" he barked, grabbing my mother around her throat.

"Leave my mother alone!" I screamed, throwing the bowl I was holding at the man.

"Shut up, little girl! Yo' mama comin' wit' me. She got work to do," he said, taking out a needle and a bag of dope, forcing my mother to shoot up.

"Why won't you let my mommy get better?

Please, leave her alone," I cried, holding on to the doll my mother got me for my birthday. All I could do was watch as the man got my mother dressed and dragged her out of the apartment, leaving me alone.

I sat on the couch and picked up the phone, still in tears. "Mrs. Duncan, it's me, Precious. Can you come upstairs and get me? My mommy had to go out and work for that mean man again."

Present...

Why did I have to go back to that day? It was one of the saddest of my life. For a brief moment, I felt how wonderful it was to spend quality time with my mother, but after that day I never saw her being drug free again. She got worse; there was no coming back. When you never know how something feels, you can't miss it; once you do, you always want it back.

I would give anything to turn back time and have my mother again. We both deserved a second chance. If I were unable to go back, then maybe I would finally join her. I felt so torn. I could see my mother's beautiful and peaceful face, but I could also hear noises and voices surrounding me.

"We're losing her. She's flat lining. No heartbeat and no pulse. Start cardiopulmonary resuscitation. If we can't get her heart back beating, she's going to die."

Aaliyah

"Grandfather, I'm so happy you're here," I said, giving him a hug. I was so relieved to see him that I tolerated the fact he brought Maya.

"How is she?"

Before I could answer grandfather's question, I heard my father yelling, trying to barge through the emergency room doors. I ran towards him to see what was going on.

"Daddy, what's wrong?"

"They're saying Precious didn't make it."

"What..." my voice cracked. "You must've misunderstood them."

"We've done everything we can."

"Then do some more. You can't let my mother

die. She can't die!" before I stood there listening to another word, I ran past everybody towards the room they were operating on mother.

"Aaliyah!" I heard my grandfather call out but I kept running, not looking back.

I burst into the room screaming, "You can't let my mother die!"

"Get her out of here," I heard one of the nurse's say.

"You better save my mother! I swear, if she doesn't make it, everyone in this room will die," I threatened.

"Get her out of here now, or she'll be arrested."

"Aaliyah, don't make things worse," my grandfather said, trying to calm me down. He was holding me closely, but all I could do was focus on what was going on in the room my mother was in. I saw them giving her chest compressions, but her monitor remained the same.

"Let's try the electric shocks one last time," I heard someone say.

I was tempted to run up on them again demanding they save my mother's life, but then something told me to start praying harder than I ever had in my entire life. So, I did. I laid my hands on the glass window and I could see my mother perfectly. She looked so at peace, it almost seemed like she was glowing.

It's not time for you to go mommy. Come back to us. We need you. Xavier needs his mother and so do I. Please, don't leave us. God, don't take my mother home with you, we need her here with us.

"Come on, Aaliyah, let's go back out to the waiting area. They're doing all they can."

"No, grandfather, you go 'head. I have to stay right here. I know you're going to think this sounds crazy, but my mother can feel my presence. She needs to in order to come back to us. I can't move. I have to stay right here."

"Then I'll stay here with you." Grandfather put his hands on my shoulders. I knew he stayed because he was worried I was about to completely lose it.

"Grandfather, look," I said, pointing towards mother. "Whatever they're doing must be working."

"Why do you say that?"

"Didn't you see? She just moved," I said, stepping back into the room. I knew I wasn't supposed to be in there, but I didn't care, I had to be as close as possible to my mother.

"Give her another electric shock, it's beginning to stimulate her heart. It's causing muscles in her chest and neck to spasm."

Within a few moments, my mother was gagging and coughing. She started reaching for the breathing tube in her throat.

"She's back," they all said, looking at the heart monitor that was no longer flat lining. I exited the room discreetly with a smile on my face.

"I think she's going to be okay," I beamed to my grandfather and dad, who were both standing right outside the door.

"I've been very lenient, but I need all of you to step off to the side. The doctor is about to come out," the nurse informed us.

"Thank you and I apologize for my outburst."

"It's your mother. I understand."

A few seconds later, the doctor came out, "How's my mother?" I asked, before he even had a chance to speak.

"We've stabilized her and given her some sedatives. She'll be on a ventilator for a few days."

"But she'll be okay, right?"

"Your mother's heart did stop for a period of time. She died, but thankfully we were able to bring her back.

"Praise the lord, she's alive," my dad said, hugging me."

"Precious is still with us, she's a fighter. Our girl is back," grandfather chimed in, and we all smiled, thanking god we had been given such a special gift today.

For the last few days, I had been walking around with no sleep. Endless consumption of caffeine was the only thing keeping my eyes open. I didn't want to leave my mother, but now that both Nico and Genesis were out the hospital and I was feeling more confident she would be okay, I came home to get some rest. I also needed to think. I had to deal with Dale and Emory and tell Nico the truth about his fiancé. I couldn't figure out how to explain to him that Ashley was really Tori and she worked for the brothers.

By now, Nico had to be trying to get in touch

with her and wondering what the hell happened. I decided to try and call Tori myself. I needed to know if she had spoken to my father at all. When I dialed her number, it was disconnected. My next call was to Dale.

"Finally, you call. I've been trying to get in touch with you for days. How's your mother?"

"Alive, but she's still on the ventilator."

"I'm so sorry, Aaliyah."

"We need to talk, but not over the phone."

"I'm sure you don't want to leave your family, so I can come to New York."

'That would be good. When can you get here?"

"Emory and I have to wrap up a couple meetings today so I can take a flight first thing tomorrow morning."

"I'll see you tomorrow." I then called Amir.

"Hey, I was just about to call you and see how you're doing?"

"I'm decent. How's Genesis?"

"He's good. I'm trying to get him to take it easy, but you know my dad."

"Of course, he's stubborn just like mine, but listen, I need to see you."

"Sure, when?"

"Can you come to my place now?"

"I have to make one stop. When I'm done, I'm on the way."

"I'll be waiting. See you soon," I said, before hanging up with Amir. My mind would not be at ease, until I found out if Dale was in cahoots with Emory in setting my family up. If he was, then without hesitation, he would die in the same manner as his brother.

Precious

"Where am I?" I mumbled quietly, trying to open my eyes.

"Daddy, she just squeezed my hand. I think she's waking up!"

"Nurse, get the doctor!"

"Where am I?" I mumbled a little louder this time.

"I can't believe it. My mom is finally waking up!"

"Aaliyah, keep your voice down, we don't want to startle her."

I could hear all these voices and conversations taking place, but it was a struggle to open my eyes and see their faces. I continued to fight to do so, because it was time and I was ready. I wanted my life back.

"Nico…where's Nico," I finally managed to say when I opened eyes.

"Mommy! I'm so happy to see you," she leaned down and kissed me on the forehead. I stared at her and then the man standing on the other side of my bed.

"Who are you people and where is Nico?"

"Doctor, something is wrong. My mother doesn't know who we are. What' going on?"

"I need both of you to step out for a minute, so I can examine my patient. "

The man and woman were hesitating. I could tell they were genuinely concerned and I wondered if they were friends of Nico's that I had never met. "What happened, am I okay?"

"You're fine," the doctor replied. "I need the two of you to leave, now," he said, turning back towards the man and woman. "I'll come out and speak with you both when I'm done." They finally left, but it was obvious to me they would've preferred to stay.

"Doctor, what is going on and why am I in the hospital?" I asked lifting my body up.

"Lay back down," he said, gently putting his hand on my shoulder, directing me to fall back. "Don't get alarmed. I'm going to ask you a few questions and answer them to the best of your ability. Okay?"

"Okay."

"Do you remember your name?"

"Of course. Precious Cummings."

"Do you remember what happened to you?"

"No, I don't."

"Do you remember where you live?"

"A brownstone in Brooklyn, but I can't remember the address. I live there with my fiancé, Nico. Is he here?"

"I'm not sure."

"Can you find out? If he isn't here, he must not know I'm in the hospital. He has to be going crazy. Please, call him, so he can come get me and take me home."

"Precious, I need you to stay in the hospital for a little longer."

"But I'm fine and I'm ready to go home."

"We need to run some more tests before you're able to go home. The nurse is going to come in and get you ready."

"Can the nurse come a little later? All of a sudden I'm feeling somewhat tired again."

"That's not a problem. You get some rest."

"Will do...and doctor?"

"Yes?"

"Please, don't let those people back in my room. I don't want to see anybody, but Nico."

"I understand."

"Thanks," I said, closing my eyes. Within seconds, I began drifting off into a deep sleep. Images of Nico and I began flashing in my mind. The first time we met, the first time we had sex, and the first time he told me he loved me. He was my everything. We were the King and Queen of Brooklyn. I began to wonder if me being in the hospital had anything to do with some street beef. So many niggas was jealous of him and wanted what he had. I couldn't help but think that maybe it was one of those low life mothefuckers that tried to take me out. It didn't matter though. Nico and I had been through so much bullshit together; we would ride this out like we did everything else.

Aaliyah

"Doctor, what is going on with my mother?"

"Yeah, doctor. My wife didn't even—I mean, my ex-wife didn't even recognize us."

"When Precious was shot, the impact her head took when she hit the concrete was extremely hard. Also, technically she died. Yes, it was for a short period of time, but she was dead. It's not uncommon for some patients, when they endure those sorts of injuries, to suffer some memory loss."

"Wait, you're saying that my mother has lost her memory?"

"Yes, it seems that way."

"But she asked for Nico," my dad said."

"That's true. She does have some memory.

How much, I'm not sure. She's resting right now, but we're going to run some more tests."

"How long will this memory loss last...a few days?" I needed to know.

"It could be a few days, a few weeks, months, years, or your mother may never fully regain her memory. In these sorts of situations, there's no telling. Like I said, we're going to monitor her, run some more tests, but honestly, only time will tell."

"Can we go see her?"

"Your mother is resting. She also informed me that the only person she wants to see is Nico. If you know how to get in touch with Nico, I suggest you get him here as soon as possible. We don't want to push her just yet. After we run the tests, then we can explain the memory loss to her; but you never know, seeing this Nico person might trigger her memory," the doctor explained, before walking off.

"This can't be happening. I get my mother back, but she doesn't even know who I am."

"Aaliyah, relax."

"How can you be so calm? It's not burning you up that's she's asking for Nico?"

"No. Honestly, I'm just relieved your mother

is alive and awake. We can work through everything else. Remember, I'm the reason she's in that condition. She was trying to save my life. If Precious had died, I would've never been able to forgive myself."

"It's not your fault mother got shot, but I promise you the people who arc responsible will pay dearly."

"Do you know who did this and if so, how?"

"No. I'm simply referring to that thing called karma. Everybody knows when you do wrong eventually you'll have to answer for it."

"That's true, but the impression I got from your statement was that you planned on handling the situation personally. I'm trying to understand how that can be." My father raised an eyebrow and stared at me with intensity.

"Daddy, you're totally taking what I said out of context. I'm a bartender for goodness sake, remember." From the cold glare Supreme was giving me, I could tell he wasn't completely buying what I was trying to sell. Luckily, my grandfather came walking up and I welcomed the distraction.

"I got your text. Precious is awake, can I go see

her?"

"She's resting, but there's a major problem, grandfather."

"What is it?"

"You tell him, dad."

"Precious, has partial memory loss."

"What, she doesn't recall the shooting? That's not surprising, especially since she just woke up."

"It's deeper than that."

"How deep?"

"Grandfather, she didn't recognize me or daddy."

"What!"

"But she did ask for Nico."

"Nico? Why the hell would she ask for him?"

"That's why I said partial memory loss because obviously, there are some people she's familiar with."

"What did the doctor say?"

"They're going to run some tests, but basically only time will tell. He also said we should get Nico here, because seeing him might trigger her memory."

"I already sent him a text. He said he was on the way," I said.

"I can't believe this shit. This family can't seem

to catch a break," my grandfather said, shaking his head.

"Quentin, the important thing is Precious is alive. Everything else will work itself out."

"How the hell can you be so calm about all this?"

"Grandfather, that's the same thing I asked him. You're taking it so well. I think it's guilt, because mom took that bullet for him."

"Supreme, you have nothing to feel guilty about. This war we've been in has been going on for over a year. First me, now your mother. Whoever's responsible, I'ma kill them myself."

"Not unless, I get to them first," I muttered.

"I didn't hear you, what did you say?"

"I just said, let's focus on mom getting better first. I'll be right back. I have to take this phone call."

"Okay, I'ma go find the doctor, so I can see what the hell is going on with my daughter," I heard grandfather say, as I was walking off.

"Amir, hi. What's the status?"

"Everything is straight. You're in the clear to make your move now."

"Excellent. I'm on it."

"Cool, I got my men on alert."

"I'll be in touch." As I was ending my call with Amir, I saw Nico coming through the door. "Dad, hi," I said, giving him a hug.

"How's your mom?"

"She woke up, so that's a good thing, but she doesn't remember who we are, but she does remember you."

"She doesn't remember anybody, but me?"

"So far, that seems to be the case. We're hoping that once she does see you, that maybe it will help the rest of her memory come back."

"Can I go see her?"

"The doctor said she fell back to sleep, but hopefully she'll wake back up soon. While we're waiting, I need to talk to you about something."

"Sure, what is it?"

"Let's go sit down." In my head, I had already decided what I would tell Nico about Tori. Everything would be the truth, except I planned on leaving out the fact I was a partner in the brother's drug operation. Since Amir promised not to divulge that information, I felt confident I could keep my secret.

"You sound serious. Is there something else

about your mother you need to tell me?"

"This isn't about mother."

"Is it you? Are you okay?"

"It's not about me, either. It's about Ashley. Have you spoken to her?"

"What made you ask about her?"

"We were supposed to meet for dinner so you could introduce me to her, but then the shooting happened."

"That's right. With all this chaos, I forgot about that," Nico said, putting his head down.

"So, have you spoken to her?"

"No, I haven't. I tried calling her after I got out the hospital and her phone was disconnected. I went to her apartment and there's no trace of her. I'm not sure, but I'm worried that she might've become a victim in this drug war we got going on. I hate thinking the worst, but you're old enough now, Aaliyah, to know how this game can go. There's always danger in every corner."

"You're right."

"Well, I'm hoping I'm wrong about Ashley. After your mother, I finally found love again for the first time and to think she could be taken away from me. That would be a hard pill to swallow."

"There's no easy way to tell you this, so I'm just gonna say it."

"Say what?"

"Ashley isn't who you think she is. Her name is really Tori."

"I'm not following you."

"She lied to you, daddy."

"Lied?"

"Yes, she was hired to infiltrate your organization."

"Aaliyah, what the hell are you talkin' about?" Nico stood up and paced the floor for a second.

"This story is so bizarre and complicated, but you have to hear it. So, I'ma give you the short version."

"Fuck that! I want the entire version and how did you find out? You don't even know her."

"That's where you're wrong. I know her very well, but I know her as Tori, not Ashley. I was lied to just like you, daddy."

"This makes no sense," he said, sitting back down next to me.

"I've been dating this guy named Dale. I never told you about him because I knew you wouldn't approve."

"Why wouldn't I approve?"

"Because he's in the same business you're in." Nico nodded his head. I could tell by his unruffled face expression he wasn't shocked by my admission.

"I see. So, what does he have to do with Ashley, or Tori? Whatever the fuck her name is."

"She was working for them. They needed her to infiltrate a competing drug operation. I was told it was for a Dominican family. When I met Tori, she was very rough around the edges. Dale asked me to clean her up. Turn her into a lady and make her appealing to a drug kingpin, so I did. Never did I suspect that drug kingpin was you."

"So, your boyfriend had you groom the woman that eventually snaked her way into my life."

"Yes," I said, swallowing hard. "The day I got to New York, Tori called me and was adamant that I met with her. That's when she told me the truth about who she was. She also told me that Emory, Dale's brother, was the one that hired her for the job. She wasn't sure if Dale was in on it, too, but I plan on finding out."

"You stay away from Dale. I'll handle him and

his brother. Where is she?"

"She wanted me to give you this," I said, reaching in my purse and taking out the diamond engagement ring. "Daddy, she said she truly fell in love with you and I believe her," I continued, before handing him the ring.

"Fuck her lies," he yelled.

"Tori's the one who warned me about the shooting at the warehouse. She did love you, daddy. She was trying to protect you."

"She knew about that?"

"She didn't know any of the details. Once Emory realized she was falling in love with you, he stopped giving her information. She eavesdropped on one of his conversations and she felt he was up to no good, and passed the info on to me."

"So, your boyfriend and his brother are responsible for that hit at the warehouse?"

"Emory is, but like I said, I don't know if Dale had any involvement."

"Aaliyah, he's the enemy. Delete him out your head the same way I'm deleting Ashley."

"Daddy, let me find out the truth first. If Dale is involved, I know that he has to go and I want him to go."

"Fine, do what you have to do, but I need to find Ashley. Nobody crosses me and gets away with it," Nico said, before tossing the diamond ring in the nearest trashcan. I was tempted to dump that wastebasket over and retrieve the ring. I knew with the size and clarity of the diamond my father had to have spent a pretty penny but at this point it represented bad luck, so I let it be. Plus, I had much bigger issues to tend to.

I had to find out the truth about what role Dale played in the hit against my family. One thing Nico was right about, at the moment he appeared to be the enemy. If that turned out to be true, my dad wouldn't have to worry about taking Dale out, because I planned on doing it myself.

Precious

"Nico, you finally came," I sighed, as I slowly started coming out of a deep sleep. "I'm ready for you to take me home." I stared at him for a moment and he seemed a little different to me, but I couldn't put my finger on it. I didn't know if all the drugs they had pumped in my system had me hallucinating or what.

"Precious, where is home?"

"What sort of silly question is that and how long have I been in this hospital?"

"Why do you ask?"

"You still look extremely good, but you seem older for some reason. I mean, I know you've always been a few years older than me, but do I see some gray hairs?" I asked, squinting my eyes trying to get a better look.

"Ha, ha, ha," Nico chuckled.

"What's so funny?"

"You are. I needed that laugh, though, but to answer your question, yes, you do see some gray hairs."

"I mean, your line of work is a hundred times more stressful than the average persons; so, I shouldn't be surprised you started getting gray hair at such a young age, but I like it. It makes you look very distinguished."

"Glad you approve. Listen, I'm going to bring your doctor in here. There are some things he needs to discuss with you."

"Things like what? I'm not paralyzed or something?" I questioned, starting to get alarmed. I immediately tried to get up out the bed to make sure my legs were still working properly and I could walk.

"Precious, lay back down," Nico said, taking my hand. "You're not paralyzed, but there are some things you need to know."

"Is it my face? Did something happen to my face?" I began rubbing my hands over my skin, making sure my features felt the same. "You're scaring me, Nico. What's wrong with me?"

"Calm down," he said, sitting down next to me. "Everything will be fine."

"You promise?"

"Of course."

"For some reason, I feel like I need you now more than ever before," I said, wrapping my arms around Nico and holding him tightly.

"I'm not going anywhere. I'll be here for you, as long as you need me."

"Did you call my mother and let her know I was in the hospital?"

"No."

"What, she went missing again? Probably on one of her drug binges," I said rolling my eyes. "I'm not giving up on her, though. I really believe in my heart she's going to get clean and stay clean one day."

"My beautiful Precious," Nico stroked my face so lovingly, "through all the tragedies, you never seem to age."

"Why are you looking at me like that?"

"Like what?"

"Like you're worried about me. And all what tragedies are you talking about? Yeah, I had a rough childhood, but damn, you make it sound like I'm not supposed to be alive."

I saw Nico's eyes scroll down to my chest. I began patting my gown and could feel the bandages underneath.

"Are you in pain?"

"No. Was I shot?" Nico nodded his head yes. "Was it bad?"

"Very."

"Did I almost die?"

"Yes."

"No wonder you're looking at me like I'm some sort of miracle child. I'm supposed to be dead."

"Let me go get the doctor." Right when Nico was standing up, the doctor walked in.

"Precious, I'm glad to see you up and alert. How are you feeling?"

"Physically I feel fine, but my fiancé has me worried. Fuck, where's my ring," I yelled, looking down at my finger. "Nico, somebody took my engagement ring."

"Nobody took your ring. I have it."

"Oh, good. I was about to wreck havoc up in this hospital."

"Nico, have you explained to Precious what happened?"

"I told her she was shot and almost died, but nothing else."

"Precious, have you begun to remember anything?"

"Not really. It's weird. I remember my childhood clearly, but only bits and pieces of the last few years. Like, I remember that Nico and I got engaged, but I can't remember where he proposed. That can't be normal."

"You suffered severe injuries and your heart also stopped for an extended period of time, so having brain trauma isn't uncommon."

"How much brain trauma did I suffer?"

"The doctor looked over at Nico, then at me, then back at Nico."

"Why the hell you keep looking at Nico? I'm the one with the brain injury. You need to explain this shit to me."

"Precious, relax."

"I won't relax until the doctor tells me what is

going on. You've been acting strange since I woke up and now the doctor acting strange. Tell me what the deal is. Whatever it is, I can handle it."

"Ms. Cummings, you have lost your memory. I'm not talking bits and pieces; I'm talking many, many years."

"How many?"

"Precious, we share a daughter who is in her early twenties."

My mouth dropped. I had to catch my breath. "No wonder you have all that gray hair." Both the doctor and Nico laughed, but the shit wasn't funny to me at all. "Is that the only child we have?"

"Yes, but you also have a younger son with Supreme."

"Who is Supreme?"

"Your ex-husband."

"So, I married somebody else besides you?"

"We never got married."

"Huh? How can that be?"

"It's a long, complicated story."

I laid my head back on the pillow. I didn't understand how I could feel one way, but I was actually somebody else. I was no longer the young teenage crazy girl who was engaged to her first love. I was a grown woman, with two children and an ex-husband.

"Doctor, will I get my memory back?"

"We're running some tests, but honestly, I don't know. Only time will tell."

"I want to see my kids. Where are they?"

"Are you sure you're up to it?" Nico asked.

"Of course. They're my blood. I want to see them."

"Aaliyah's right outside. If I'm not mistaken, Xavier is with Supreme's parents."

"I see. Doctor, can you have my daughter come in."

"Sure, I'll be right back."

"Precious, you don't have to push yourself."

"I'm fine. I may not remember them, but trust me I need my kids. You and them are what's gonna get me through this. I know you said we never married, does that mean you married somebody else?"

"No, I've never been married."

"What happened between us? Forget it, I don't want to know. All I need to know is if you're going to stay by my side through this, because in my heart, what I remember is still being very much in love with you."

Nico reached over and put his hand on top of mine. "I told you I wasn't going anywhere. We'll get through this together, I promise."

"Mom, how are you?" Nico and I both turned towards the door at the same time.

"You must be Aaliyah," I smiled. "You were here earlier with that man. I thought they were friends of yours, Nico. I'm so sorry for brushing you off."

"You don't have to apologize. I'm just so happy to see you. Can I give you a hug?"

"Of course, you're my daughter and what a beautiful daughter you are," I said, squeezing her tightly.

"I know you don't remember me, but I have enough love for the both of us," Aaliyah said, with tears in her eyes.

"I do love you. You have my mother's name and her eyes. She must adore you."

Aaliyah looked over at Nico then back at me. "I've never met my grandmother."

"My mother. Is she dead?" Aaliyah's and Nico's

silence gave me my answer. So many things had changed and the only good things seemed to be my children. I wondered what all had happened in these last twenty something years. Maybe losing my memory was a blessing in disguise. This could be a new beginning for me, to right the wrongs of my past and begin a new journey. At the moment, I was filled with confusion. The only thing I was confident about was that as long as I had my kids and Nico by my side, I would come through this stronger and better than before.

Aaliyah

"Come in." As I stood face to face with Dale, I wondered if this would be the last time I'd see him alive, but all of that simply depended on him.

"You haven't seen me in weeks and this is the greeting I get? Where's my hug and kiss?"

Seeing Dale again had taken longer than I planned, which was due to Amir. When I asked him to assist me with finding out if Dale was working with Emory to bring my family down, Amir thought what I needed him to do would only take a few days to get done. But after calling me to say everything was a go, he realized there was a slight problem and he needed more time. I then had to call Dale and postpone him coming to New York, but with my mother getting out the hospital, that was easy to justify. Now that Amir was finally able to get what I needed done, it was do or die time for Dale.

"Honestly, after what I found out I don't think I'll ever be able to kiss you again," I said, skipping the kiss, but giving Dale a half ass hug. The only reason I hugged him was to check to see if he was carrying a weapon, which he wasn't. Since he was coming to see me, Dale probably left his gun in the car, thinking it would be a love fest between us, but he was sorely mistaken.

After my dry hug, Dale leaned his head back as if sizing me up before responding. "Are you joking or are you serious? I can't really tell right now."

"I'm very serious. Come, have a seat. Can I get you anything to drink?"

"No, I'm good. I'm more interested in finding out where all this coldness is coming from."

Once Dale was comfortably seated, I sat down on the chair across from him. I had my gun under one of the pillows, in case I had to shoot him right on the spot. I was hoping it wouldn't come to that, mainly because I didn't want to ruin my brand new furniture with his blood, but that could always be replaced. If my plan played out the way I suspected, Dale wouldn't be killed until after he left my place, which was ideal.

"Have you spoken to Tori?"

"So, that's what this is about. How did you find out?"

"She told me. So, it's true," I said, reaching under the pillow to retrieve my gun, ready to start blasting without the conversation having to go any further.

"You talk to Tori? When? We can't get in touch with her."

"Oh, so, what did you mean 'that's what this is about?'" I asked, easing up on the trigger.

"You found out Tori is missing and you're upset that I didn't inform you. Don't be mad. I knew you were going crazy over your mother and I didn't want you stressing about business. Wait, you saying you spoke Tori?"

"Yes, I did."

"When?"

"The day my family was ambushed and my mother almost died."

"That was weeks ago. You haven't spoken to

her since?"

"No. Tori told me she was going on the run. She needed to disappear."

"Why and why are you just telling me this? Or is this what you needed to speak with me about?"

"Yes. Tori informed me that your brother hired her to infiltrate my family, so he could take them down. Instead of her seducing the Dominican kingpin, she actually seduced my father, Nico Carter. It worked because they got engaged. She explained that she actually fell in love with him and wanted me to know the truth, before she left town."

"What in the fuck!"

"And the only reason you're not dead already is because Tori wasn't sure if you knew what your brother was up to."

"So, wait, you think I had something to do with the hit on your people," Dale said, rising up.

"Sit down," I ordered, but I didn't show my weapon yet. I wasn't ready for him to know there was a possibility he was about to die.

"Aaliyah, don't do this," Dale said, as if sensing time was running out for him.

"Sit down!"

"I understand you're pissed the fuck off. I would be too, but on everything I hold dear to me, which includes you, I had absolutely nothing to do with what happened to your family."

"Then call Emory right now."

"Huh?"

"You heard me. Get on your phone and call Emory. Put it on speaker. Don't let him know you're with me."

"And say what?"

"Tell him that you believe I spoke to Tori and she told me everything. You want to know how he thinks I should be dealt with."

Dale looked down at the Macassar Ebony hardwood floor completely mute. He lifted his arms, resting his elbows on his upper legs, before folding his hands and placing them under his chin. His thoughts had taken him elsewhere.

"What's the hesitation, Dale? Are you placing the call or not?"

"There are a couple of reasons for the hesitation. Besides you believing I'm your enemy, there might be a chance my brother is and that concerns me."

"I know for a fact that Emory is behind this bullshit, now I just need to know if you are, too."

"You know for a fact based on something Tori told you? How the fuck you know she ain't lying?"

"It is no secret how your brother feels about me. It would be classic Emory to use me to train the woman who is going to fuck my father."

"Yeah, Emory may have his issues with you, but he respects business and more importantly, he respects me. My brother knows how I feel about you. I don't believe he would cross me like that."

"But you're not sure. Just like I'm not sure if this whole spill you're giving me is some bullshit. So, are you going to call your brother or not?"

Without saying another word, Dale took out his cell and called Emory. He put the call on speaker and we both listened as the phone rang. Emory answered on the fourth ring.

"What up bruh."

"We have a situation."

"What the fuck happened now?"

"It's Tori."

"Don't tell me she ended up on a dead end street."

"Not that I know of."

"Then what?" Dale paused for a second and glanced over at me. I nodded my head letting him know to speak that shit.

"I believe Tori spoke to Aaliyah and told her everything."

"Everything like what?"

"About you setting her family up. Using Tori to get next to Aaliyah's pops."

"Yo, what the fuck are you talkin' 'bout?"

"Don't act like you don't know what's up. Tori told Aaliyah that you had her get next to her father, so you could bring down her family."

"That's some straight bullshit, but yo' let me call you back."

"Why? Let's finish this up now."

" Just let me call you back."

"How long?"

"Give me twenty minutes."

"Okay."

"Are you satisfied," Dale said, once he ended the call.

"Hell no."

"You still believe I had something to do with

this?"

"I'm not one hundred percent sure you didn't."

"I'm telling you I didn't and after that conversation with my brother, I don't believe Emory did, either. I know when he's lying and he was telling me the truth."

"That's not good enough."

"Damn, I swear I thought we were better than this," Dale said, punching his fist in the palm of his hand. "Listen, just give me a little time."

"What you mean."

"Let me try to clear my name and my brother's name."

"How you plan on doing that?"

"Finding out who really set your family up, because it damn sure wasn't me and it wasn't my brother, either."

"Why shouldn't I just kill you now?"

"Because if you do, you'll never find out the truth."

"Fine, but I think you better go, before I change my mind."

"So, it's like that?"

"For now, yes. Let's just hope it doesn't get

worse. Goodbye, Dale."

"I'ma prove you wrong. Not only 'cause we business partners, but also because I have real feelings for you. If I can't earn your trust, then we have nothing."

"Just go."

In the back of Dale's mind, I knew he had to be wondering why I let him go. He probably thought it was because I had love for him and although I did, that wasn't the reason. If I truly believed Dale was in on my family's hit, I would've killed him right on the spot, but I still wasn't sure, though I would know very soon. See, the reason Emory wanted to call Dale back was because he had another phone he used that nobody really knew about, but I did and it was because of Amir.

Amir had an inside connect that could place a phone tap if he had certain information on the person. I gave Amir both phone numbers I had on Emory but when one of his workers did some deep digging, he realized Emory had another phone he used primarily to discuss the most critical issues when it came to business. It took some time and maneuvering to get that number, which caused a delay with my plan.

I was positive Emory would be calling Dale back on that phone and I would be able to hear all the details. That conversation would either save Dale's life or have both brothers ending up in body bags.

Precious

For the last couple of weeks, Nico's home had become like Grand Central Terminal. People were constantly coming in and out, and it was mostly to visit me and see how I was doing. Initially, Nico was limiting my visitors, but I was feeling stronger with each passing day, and I was ready to deal with everybody that had played a role in my life, before the accident. That's why when I heard Nico and Quentin arguing about me, I decided to listen, before making my presence known.

"Quentin, Precious is just getting to know you again, so let that shit play out before you start trying to bring Maya up in here."

"Maya is her sister. Precious has every right to

get to know her, too."

"Cut the bullshit. You know damn well Precious and Maya have never had no type of sister relationship. You're trying to use Precious' memory loss to ignite a link between them and frankly, I don't like it. Precious loathes Maya and just because she can't remember that shit don't mean it still ain't true."

"Man, you a damn walking hypocrite."

"What are you talkin' 'bout?"

"Before Precious lost her memory, she was in love with two men and neither one of them were you. So, if we're to go by what you're saying regarding Maya, then Precious needs to be out of your house and go back to either Lorenzo or Supreme. Because we both know that before her accident, she wasn't checking for you."

"I want the two of you stop," I said, walking into the living room. I had heard enough and I didn't want this shit escalating any further.

"Precious, how much of the conversation did you hear?"

"Enough to know your conversation needed to end. Nico, I appreciate you trying to protect me, but I want to meet everybody that had an impact in my life. Like the doctor said, we don't know who might trigger my memory coming back."

"But you hate Maya."

"She used to hate Maya," Quentin said, frowning at Nico, before turning his attention to me. "Maybe this will be a blessing to both of you. Precious, because you can no longer remember the bad blood between you and your sister, you might finally be open to working on building a relationship."

"You've always been so determined for them to bond. Maybe you need to just let that shit go."

"Nico, they share the same blood. They family. Of course I want my two daughters to bond, what father wouldn't? Plus, Maya has changed. She deserves a second chance and maybe now Precious will give it to her. Will you do that?"

"Yes, I will. My mother's gone. I don't have a lot of family. I want to get to know my sister."

"Thank you," Quentin said, before coming over and giving me a hug. "This means the world to me. Before I leave this earth, I want my girls to share a solid connection."

"Nothing like seeing father and daughter embracing."

"Genesis, I didn't even hear you come in."

"The maid let me in. I guess with all the commotion going on in here, nobody heard the doorbell."

"Yeah, things were a bit heated," Nico commented, still annoyed.

"Hopefully you all got everything resolved. Precious, you seem more and more like yourself each time I come. I can see that fire in your eyes again."

"Really?"

"Yep. It's good to see, too. Out of all your great qualities, your fiery personality is one of my favorites."

"Mine, too," Quentin smiled.

"I think we all can agree we appreciate that fire in Precious, but Genesis, I'm sure you didn't come all the way to Jersey to tell us that," Nico shrugged, unable to let go of the bad mood his disagreement with Quentin put him in.

"You're right. I'm actually here because we've made some movement tracking Ashley down."

"Who is Ashley?" I noticed all three men look at each other, but nobody was answering my question. “Who the fuck is Ashley, and don’t ignore my question.”

“We think she knows who ordered the hit at the warehouse.”

“You mean the warehouse where I almost died,” I snapped. “And all of you are standing there like you don’t want to include me in what the fuck is going on. That’s not gonna happen. I want to be kept in the loop with all this shit. Whoever is responsible will answer to me. Are we clear?”

“Precious, I just think...”

“I’m not asking you to think,” I said, cutting Nico off. I’m telling you that I will play a major role in bringing down everybody that was responsible for what happened to me. So, Genesis, tell me more.”

“Amir had a wiretap put on Emory’s phone.”

“Who is Emory? I need to be caught up on all these people.”

“Emory is the brother of Aaliyah’s boyfriend Dale.”

“Our daughter has a boyfriend and we’re taping his brother’s phone. This is complicated and getting very interesting. I see you all have been keeping me in the dark about a lot of things.”

"Precious, I'll fill you in on all the details later on. Genesis, just tell us about Ashley," Nico said.

"Ashley has a brother that lives in L.A., and supposedly, when she left New York, she might have gone to stay with him. I got the address and I'm leaving tomorrow to go track her down, before Emory or his brother can get to her."

"I'm coming with you," Nico said.

"So am I and I don't want to hear a word from any of you. I'm going and that's final."

"The jet is taking off at nine in the morning. I'll see you both there. Don't be late," Genesis, said, before leaving.

"Pretty girl, you be careful on this trip. Call me if you need me. When you get back, I want us to have dinner with Maya. Okay?"

"Okay, and thank you," I said, giving Quentin a kiss on the cheek.

"Genesis, hold up. I need to speak to you," Quentin said, catching up to Genesis, as they both left out.

"Why are you standing over there with an attitude?" I asked Nico, who was staring out of the vast windows that had a skyline view of NYC. Both hands were in his pockets and he still seemed to be pissed off.

"I need to tell you something before we go to L.A., tomorrow."

"Tell me what?"

"The woman Ashley we're looking for."

"What about her?"

"She was my fiancé."

"How long ago?"

"Up until the day you were shot. Even after that."

"What! You were engaged to the woman that had something to do with me almost getting killed. You and Genesis also getting shot and let's not forget about some of our workers that were killed during the shootout."

"Yo, don't you think I know that shit. I had no idea that the woman I wanted to spend the rest of my life with was a fuckin' snake ass traitor."

"You wanted to spend the rest of your life with her?"

"Yeah, that's what being engaged and getting married usually means."

"Fuck you, you smartass sonofabitch. I guess I just thought I was the only woman you had ever wanted to spend the rest of your life with."

"Believe it or not, I had a fuckin' life after you. Did you expect for me to wait for you forever? Even after your marriage ended with Supreme, you still didn't come back to me. Instead, you started some bullshit affair with Lorenzo, who also happened to be one of my business partners. But what Precious wants, Precious has to have, no matter who it hurts. Developing into a grown woman didn't even make you become less self-centered."

"Why don't you tell me how you really feel, Nico," I said folding my arms. "I guess we weren't on the best of terms before I got shot."

"We were actually finally getting to a good place again, but it took some time. As much as I always wanted you back, I could deal with you being with Supreme. I came to accept you chose him and the two of you belonged together, but then when it came out that you were having an affair with Lorenzo," Nico turned away and there was a long pause before he continued, "for a very long time I was angry with you."

"It sounds like you still are."

"I think I'm more so angry with myself."

"Why?"

"Because after all the bullshit, I never stopped loving you and there were many times I wanted to, but you were it for me."

"What about this Ashley woman?"

Nico sat down on the couch, before answering. He was silent, as if getting his thoughts together. "Ashley seemed almost too good to be true and that's because she was. All of the traits that made me drawn to her were the ones just like yours. That's because our daughter had been unwittingly used to train her for that very purpose. So, I never fell in love with Ashley. I fell in love with the idea of her being you."

"You don't need a carbon copy of me anymore. I'm yours, if you still want me."

"I never stopped wanting you, but what's going to happen when your memory comes back? Right now, you think you're in love with me, but that will change."

"Honestly, I don't even want to consider that. Of course I would love to remember the things in my past, but not if that means giving up you. I don't want my heart to stop loving you, because it feels so right to me. My mind, body, and soul only yearn for you, and it's the most amazing feeling. I feel like a teenager all over again. I still remember the first time we made love. I keep playing it over and over in my head, but I want to create new memories. Can we start now?"

"Are you sure you're ready for that? I don't want you to feel like I'm taking advantage of you."

"I want you to take advantage of me," I laughed. "Seriously, I need to feel you inside of me again," I said, softly kissing his right earlobe. I remembered it was one of Nico's hot spots. "It's the only way I'm going to feel truly alive," I whispered in his ear.

"Say no more." Nico lifted me up and carried me upstairs. We had been sleeping in separate bedrooms, but when he laid me down on his bed, I knew this would be where I'd stay for good.

Nico kept staring directly in my eyes the entire time he was undressing me. It was as if he was penetrating my soul. I leaned up from the bed to kiss him, but he shook his head as if to say no.

"Why won't you kiss me?"

"I just want to stare at you for a moment. I've

wanted you for so long. I never believed we would be together like this again. I need to know it's real," Nico said, as his fingers caressed every inch of my body. Then he raised my legs, kissing the inside of my thighs, before his tongue licked me from the very front to the very back of my wet pussy. I held on to the silk sheets as my body was in complete ecstasy. I felt like my cherry was being popped for the very first time.

Once Nico slid inside of me, I wrapped my legs around him, wanting to feel every inch of his manhood. He still felt just as good as the very first time we made love. I was finally back home where I belonged and I welcomed it.

Aaliyah

"It looks like your boyfriend was telling the truth," Amir mocked.

"You sound disheartened. Did you want Dale to be responsible for what happened to my mother?"

"I didn't say that."

"Yeah, but your tone did. What I'm most surprised about is that Emory wasn't involved, either."

"Yeah, you've heard all of Emory's phone conversations for the last few weeks and we got nothing. He certainly feels just as duped by that Tori chick as you do."

"Yep, but I'm fuckin' pissed that we weren't able to go to L.A.. We were the ones that got the information about Tori's brother. Plus, I want that trick to pay for lying to me. I believed her when she said Emory put her up to seducing my father, but it was all lies. She knew we didn't like each other and used that to her advantage."

"True or maybe blaming Emory was the better option."

"What do you mean?"

"Maybe she wanted to come clean and try to protect Nico, but was too afraid to tell you who she was really working for."

"But Emory isn't somebody to fuck with. He can be extremely lethal. If what you're thinking is true, then whoever this other person is must be some sort of monster."

"The only way we're going to find out is by talking to Tori."

"Exactly. So, are you coming with me or not?"

"Coming with you where?"

"Where do you think? L.A.. Are you coming or do you need to get permission from Latreese?"

"This has nothing to do with Latreese. My father said they would handle it. I think we should respect that."

"We won't interfere. We'll just be there for backup support. So, are you in?"

"Yeah, if only to watch over you and make sure you don't fuck anything up."

"Cool. I'll make our reservations. We'll take the red-eye. I'll text you the information."

"Alright."

"And, Amir, don't tell your dad we're coming," I smiled, before closing the door behind him.

I headed to my bedroom to start packing my clothes. I was looking forward to this trip. Not only because I couldn't wait to get my hands on Tori, but also because I hated being in this apartment by myself. My mom was staying with Nico, in Jersey, so it was just me in this massive crib. It was beautiful and in a great location, but it would be better if my mother was here with me. I was tempted to go stay with them in Jersey, but when Supreme and my little brother came to town, I knew it would be awkward for them to have to come to Nico's house to see me. Plus, I still wasn't comfortable with the idea of them being together as a couple. My entire life, I never saw them that way. They were always just my parents. As far as I was concerned, my mother belonged with

Supreme. As I was getting caught up in my thoughts, I heard the door.

"That must be Amir again," I said, tossing my tote bag down and heading to the front door. "Did you forget something, because if you came back to try and convince me not to go on this trip, you're wasting your time," I yelled out as I was opening the door. "What tha fuck!" I screamed, seeing a man with a black ski mask on, standing in front of me.

I quickly tried to slam the door shut, but he was too strong and pushed it back open. I began hauling ass, but the man grabbed my ponytail, yanking my head back. I fell to the floor and I saw him reaching in his pocket for a rag. I could smell the chloroform as he tried to cover my nose. With all my strength, I was clawing at his face, but his strength was overpowering me. I finally maneuvered my legs in a position to knee him right in his dick. I pushed up so hard, not once but twice. I had that nigga howling like a hit dog. In his moment of weakness, I got up and ran to my bedroom. I heard him coming up behind me, but by then I had already retrieved my gun.

I started busting off shots and it seemed like

the assailant literally flew up out of the apartment. I ran after him ready to fire off some more shots, but he had vanished. The motherfucker was hurt. There were traces of blood in the hallway and outside my apartment door. Somebody was after me and I suspected it was the same fucks who almost killed my mother.

Precious

"We've been to that house three times and nobody has been there. Maybe the information Amir got was wrong or maybe Tori and her brother left, but I think this is a bust," I said to Nico and Genesis, as we sat in The Blvd restaurant, at the Beverly Wilshire Hotel, having breakfast.

"You might be right, Precious. We can send one of our men here to watch the property for a couple of weeks, while we check into other leads."

"Sounds good to me."

"Let's do one last visit. If we come up empty,

then we'll proceed like you suggested, Genesis."

"Can't hurt, let's get out of here."

After paying the bill, we headed back out to Beverlywood. When we arrived to the tree-lined street on Monte Mar Drive, nothing had changed. The house appeared to be vacant.

"There's nothing here for us to see," I huffed, frustrated with this entire excursion. Not wanting this trip to be a complete bust, I was hoping to spend time with my son, but Xavier and Supreme had recently arrived on the east coast. That was the main reason I wanted to end this trip, because I was anxious to get back home and be with my son, again. I had only seen him a handful of times, since getting out of the hospital and knowing he wasn't in L.A. right now, made my patience level for this city zero.

"I agree. There's no sense in spending anymore time here."

"Did either one of you notice that Maserati parked across the street? Is hasn't been here the last three times we came," Nico commented.

"So, what's your point?"

"It seems a tad out of place on this street."

"There are some very nice homes over here.

What do you mean out of place?"

"Yes a lot of the cars over here are nice, but not that flashy."

"Maybe they're visiting somebody in the neighborhood."

"Genesis, drive by that car slowly as we're leaving."

"I doubt anybody is sitting in the car, Nico."

"We're about to find out."

Genesis made his way down the street and when we got closer to the Maserati, he began to slow down. "Isn't this special," Nico said, rolling down his window.

"What the hell are the two of you doing here? Aaliyah, does your grandfather know you left town?"

"Mother, I'm not twelve years old. I don't have to get permission to leave town."

"I thought I told you to let us handle this," Genesis said to Amir.

"That was the plan, but Aaliyah had other ideas. I couldn't let her come to L.A. by herself."

"Neither one of you should be here."

"I think I should be here when you all talk to Tori. I think I can help get the necessary information from her."

"Well, you wasted your time coming. This is our fourth trip to this house and nobody has been there. I'm thinking this is either the wrong address, or the info you all got is suspect."

"This is the right address," Amir insisted. "Maybe somehow Tori got word that we located her at this address, so she and her brother left."

"Don't look now, but the house finally has a visitor," Aaliyah said. "Okay, now look."

We all turned our head to face the house and saw a woman going inside. From the distance we couldn't get a good look of who it was but we all intended to find out.

"What ya' waiting for...move," Nico barked. Genesis parked our car behind Amir's and we all headed towards the house.

"Nico and Amir, you all go around and guard the back exit. We'll take the front," Genesis directed. They nodded their heads and took off. "Precious, you ring the doorbell. I'll stand off the side and when she opens the door, that's when I'll move in. Aaliyah..."

"I know. I won't say a word."

"Alright, let's move."

I rang the doorbell, but no one answered. I began knocking and still no answer. I thought I saw a woman walk by, so I started talking loudly through the door.

"Can I please use your phone? I just moved a few doors down and I locked myself out. I left my cell phone in the house. Please help."

A few moments later I heard the door opening. When it reached the halfway point, Genesis stepped out from hiding, pushing the door open with the tip of his gun.

"Please don't shoot!" the woman cried out.

"Is there anyone else here?" Genesis asked.

"No it's just me. I was coming to get a few things. Don't kill me."

"Sit down over there," Genesis said, pointing the gun towards a couch in a sitting area. "Aaliyah, go let Nico and Amir in."

"What do you want from me?"

"If you answer a few questions truthfully, we might let you live."

I stared at the woman and she appeared harmless. A very pretty lady that looked no more than thirty. She was dressed casually in some fitted jeans, Ugg boots, and a white cami.

"Whatever you want to know I'll tell, but I don't want to die."

"Where the hell is Ashley?" Nico asked, storming in the room as if on a kill mission.

"I don't know an Ashley," the woman stuttered, clearly fearing for her life.

"He means Tori," Aaliyah said, giving the correct name. The woman's face expression changed when Aaliyah gave that name. She swallowed hard and I noticed her hands shaking.

"I suggest you tell us what you know, before things get ugly," I advised.

"I don't know Tori that well, but I used to be very close to her brother."

"Isn't this her brother's house?"

"It was."

"It was until when? And if he no longer lives here, what are you doing here?"

"It was up until a week ago, when Gregory was killed."

"Tori's brother is dead?"

"Yes. He was leaving his office in Beverly Hills and somebody shot him in his head, when he was getting in his car."

"Did it have anything to do with his sister?"

"I think so. I used to date Gregory about a year ago. Although we weren't together, we remained good friends. He told me his Tori had gotten into some trouble and she was coming to stay with him. Next thing I know, Gregory is dead."

"Again, why are you here?" Nico questioned, as if uninterested in the woman's sad story.

"Tori called earlier today and asked me to stop by Greg's house to pick up some of her stuff. Once he got killed, she stopped staying and she didn't want to come back. I still had a key to his place, so I told her no problem."

"Give us the address where Tori's staying."

"I don't know it."

"Don't lie to me!"

"Nico, calm down," I said, watching his anger elevate.

"I swear! I've seen her once since she came back to L.A., and that was weeks ago."

"So, how is she supposed to get her stuff from you?"

"She said she would call me later on, to tell me where to meet her."

Nico grabbed the woman's purse and pulled out her wallet. He opened it and reached for her driver's license, studying the information. "Skylar, I guess we'll all be waiting together because you're not going anywhere, until I get my hands on Tori," he said, tossing her belongings down on the table.

"I have a mother that loves me and a little boy that needs me. My son is only two. I haven't done anything wrong. I don't know what Tori is involved in, but it has nothing to do with me."

I didn't want to say it out loud, but I wasn't feeling good about this. Maybe it was because of my near death experience, but the fear in the woman's voice was eating my insides up. I was all for everybody dying that had something to do with the hit at the warehouse, but not innocent people losing their lives, especially not a mother. I couldn't live with that, particularly since I had been given a second chance with my own life.

"Skylar, help us find Tori, and you can go home to your son. I promise you that."

"Don't make promises you can't keep, Precious."

"I intend on keeping that promise. We have no reason to kill her, if she delivers Tori. That's the reason why we're here."

"This is my problem to deal with. You follow my lead."

"Oh really? I'm the one that almost died and lost my fuckin' memory. If anybody has a bone to pick, it's me, Nico."

"Both of you, that's enough," Genesis interjected. "We all want the same thing. Going at each other isn't going to make it happen any quicker. So, everybody settle down. Skylar, you don't have an address on Tori, but you do have a phone number...correct?"

"Yeah, I think the number she's been calling me on is her cell."

"Call her. Let her know you got her stuff and you want to meet with her now."

"Okay," Skylar said, reaching in her purse for her phone.

"Put the call on speaker," Nico said, while we all stood silently, waiting for Tori to answer.

"Hello."

"Hey, Tori. I got the stuff you wanted. The thing is, I just got a call that I have to go out of town for a job. I wanted to give you your belongings before I left. Can you meet up now?"

"Umm, I'm kinda in the middle of something. Can you give me an hour?" Skylar looked up at Nico, who nodded his head yes.

"Sure. Where?" There was a brief moment of silence, as if Tori were thinking of a place to meet.

"What about that gas station around the corner from my brother's house? You know, the one he used to always go to."

"Yeah, I know exactly where you're talking about." I could tell from their somber tone, both women were sharing a moment of sadness over Tori's brother.

"So, I'll see you there in an hour, but I'll send you a text confirming I'm on the way."

"Cool, see you then." After Skylar ended her call, she looked up at Genesis. "I did my part, can I go now?"

"What are you, stupid....hell no!"

"Nico, it's not necessary to call her names, but no, Skylar, you can't leave."

"Sure the fuck not. Yo' ass going to the gas station to meet her."

"It's obvious you all are going to do something really bad to Tori. Although we're not close, I don't want to see it go down."

"I understand, but that's not your decision to make. Until we no longer need you, you'll do as we say," Genesis made clear.

I was starting to get the feeling that maybe I did make Skylar a promise I would be unable to keep. I knew Nico didn't care if the woman had to die, but I was getting the sense that Genesis didn't care either. If that was the case, nobody could save Skylar, including me.

Aaliyah

"Mom, are you okay?"

"Why do you ask me that?"

"You might've lost your memory, but your gestures, the facial expressions you make when you're reacting to something, are the same."

"I'm that transparent?"

"Not to everybody, but to me, yes. You're my mother and I know you. I can tell when something is bothering you."

"I think your father and Genesis are going to kill that woman," my mom said, glancing over at Skylar. She was sitting up on the couch in the fetal position, with the most distraught look on her face. It was as if Skylar also knew she was going to be killed.

"I think you're right and honestly, I don't think she should die either, but what choice do we have? She can identify us. After we get Tori, what if she goes to the police?"

"I don't think she will. She has a little boy. She doesn't want those types of problems for her family. If we kill Tori, she knows we'll come back and kill her, too."

"I hear you, but convincing dad and Genesis of that is a different story. If I had to pick one for you to reason with, I would say talk to Genesis."

"I agree. That hour mark is quickly approaching, so if I'm gonna make some headway with Genesis, I better start now. I'll be back. Wish me luck."

"You and your mother seemed to be having a heavy conversation," Amir said, coming up to me after my mom had walked off. "Were you telling her what happened to you right before we came to L.A.?"

"Are you crazy? If my parents knew what went down, they would have me under twenty-four hour surveillance."

"Maybe you need to be. At least, until we find out who's behind it."

"I'm sure it's the same person or people behind this bullshit with our family, but obviously they wanted to kidnap me and not kill me, the reason for the chloroform. I wondered if they planned on holding me for some sort of ransom. All this shit is bizarre."

"That's why we need to tell our parents, so we can figure this out."

"Amir, I'll let you know when it's the right time to tell our parents. If you're so concerned about my well-being, just watch over me until we do," I remarked.

"The text just came," Genesis said, holding up Skylar's phone. "Tori will be at the gas station in fifteen minutes. I'll ride with Skylar. You all stay close behind, but far enough that Tori can't see you."

"Are we going to snatch Tori up at the gas station, or follow her to her next destination, before making a move?" I asked.

"At the gas station. We can't take any chances that she might get away. Once Skylar and Tori make the exchange, Nico, that's when you grab her and put Tori in the car, with you and Precious. Then, we'll all meet up at the spot in Culver City. Are we clear?"

"Yep, we all said in unison."

"Then, let's go."

"What's gonna happen to me?" we all turned towards Skylar. Her eyes were filled with tears and fear.

"We'll figure that out later," Genesis said, before we all headed out.

"How did your talk go with Genesis?" I questioned my mother on the low, while we were going to our cars.

"Not sure. He seemed resistant to the idea of letting her live. There is still time for Genesis to change his mind, but I doubt he will," my mother said, before getting in the car with Nico.

I knew death was part of the game we were in, but it never got easy watching blameless people become casualties of drug wars. Seeing Skylar get in that car with Genesis, knowing her life was coming to an end because of Tori's reckless decisions, was even difficult for me to accept. Skylar's son would grow up without a mother, because of somebody else's sin. Life truly could be fucked up.

"Park over there," I told Amir, when we pulled into the McDonald's parking lot right next to the gas station. We were out of sight, but had a great view of everything. Soon after, Nico drove up and parked beside us. From the short distance, we watched and waited for Tori to come.

"Tori should've been here twenty minutes ago. You think she found out something was up with Skylar and bailed?"

"I hope not. Skylar must be sittin' in that car 'bout to lose her mind. When she agreed to do Tori a favor, never did she think it would turn into this fiasco."

"I sent my dad a text asking him what was up, but got nothing. Look at the tinted Camry pulling into the gas station. Do you think that could be Tori?"

"Nope, not unless Tori morphed into a Hispanic man. Don't fret, we hit the jackpot. Peep the Cherokee. The woman behind the wheel looks like Tori to me. My dad must think so, too," I said, watching him driving away from McDonald's, headed towards the gas station.

A few seconds later, Skylar got out of the car with a bag of Tori's stuff. The women seemed to be exchanging words and gave each other a quick hug, before going back to their cars. That's when Nico went into motion. He stormed towards Tori, while my mother waited in the front seat, ready to drive off, once she was snatched up.

What happened next was like watching a horror scene play out in a movie. Another car came out of nowhere and the Hispanic man that was in the Camry reappeared, armed and firing shots. Before I could say 'what the fuck', bullets were flying everywhere. In the midst of Skylar running towards her car, she tripped and fell. Genesis jumped out and began busting shots to cover Skylar, so she wouldn't get shot, but Tori wasn't so lucky. It was evident the men came specifically for her, because they lit her ass up. Her body was riddled with bullets. As quickly as the goons appeared, they vanished, leaving a bloodied and very dead Tori. Luckily, nobody else was hurt in the mayhem.

Precious

"Somebody wanted to shut Tori up and they succeeded. Now, we're right back where we started," I said, observing the defeated expression on Nico's face.

"I still can't believe I saw Tori die right in front of my face. It would've been me, too, if it wasn't for you, Genesis. I know I said it before, but thank you. You saved my life," Skylar cried, hugging Genesis. To my surprise he hugged her back.

"So, what do we do next?" Aaliyah asked, as we all sat around at the stash house in Culver City, trying to figure out how to fix this shit.

"We need to go back home. There is nothing left in L.A. for us," Nico said, breaking his silence.

"I agree with Nico. Tori was our link. Now

that she's dead, we need to get the hell out of here. These streets of L.A. are hot. There's no telling if they plotting on us right now. I say we get back to our turf. We can call in some help here, but we got much stronger backup in New York." After Genesis made his stance clear, I noticed Skylar saying some things to him in a low voice.

"Genesis, can I speak to you for a minute?"

"What's up?" he said, following me in the kitchen.

"I couldn't help but notice the interaction between you and Skylar. A couple hours ago, you planned on killing her, now you're exchanging hugs. What brought about the one-eighty?"

"You were right. She didn't deserve to die."

"That's true, but that doesn't mean I expected the two of you to bond."

"Saving somebody's life can have that affect."

"Why did you save her life?"

"When we were in the car waiting for Tori, she showed me pictures of her son and her mother. She talked to me about her life and struggles. She's a good girl."

"You like her, don't you?"

"Would I be wrong if I said yes?"

"Not at all. There was something I liked about her, too. She has a sweetness about her, but there lies the problem, she's too sweet. A woman like Skylar doesn't fit into our lifestyle."

"She understands the struggle."

"That's where you're wrong. Her struggle is not our type of struggle. I can tell by the look in her eyes. She's not 'bout this life. Do you really want to be responsible for turning a good girl bad?"

"No, I don't."

"I didn't think so. That's why we need to get on this jet and you leave Skylar right where you found her, in L.A."

Genesis left out the kitchen with displeasure written on his face. I felt bad for him. I didn't understand how a man as fine as Genesis and with all his money was single. Plus, he had such an endearing spirit. I would think he'd have women lined up. Because I had no memory of him, I asked Nico to fill me in. He explained that Genesis was a complete workaholic. For years, he focused on raising his son and making money. Now that Amir was grown, he must've desired the company of a good woman, but in our line of business you didn't come across many of those. Skylar was probably like a breath of fresh air for him. She represented everything that seemed out of reach: a beautiful regular chick, with regular problems, living a regular life. The problem was there was nothing regular about us. Skylar would never fit in and Genesis knew it.

"You didn't say a word the entire flight or on the ride home. Are you gonna tell me what's bothering you?"

"You know what the fuck is bothering me. Somebody is out to destroy us and the one person who could tell us who it is, is dead."

"True, but I think it's more to it than that."

"More like what?"

"Maybe you're mourning Tori's death. You all were engaged."

"Are you fuckin' serious? She was a snake."

"True, but a snake that loved you. It had to be hard watching her die."

"Did you not forget I planned on killing her myself, once we got the information we needed."

"Nico, you don't have to pretend to be so cold.

It's okay to admit that you loved her and you were hurt."

"I explained to you what I felt for Tori wasn't love. She was a bootleg version of you. I hated that ho after I found out what she did. Tori was a fraud and I wanted her dead." Nico walked over to the bar and poured himself a drink, before continuing. "Precious, you need to understand something about me: I am cold. With your memory loss, you only remember the good things about us, but there was a lot of bad."

"I don't want to hear about the bad. Maybe I forgot for a reason."

"You need to hear it. If we gon' move forward, I want you to understand who I am."

"I do know who you are and I love you, regardless. So, I don't think you're cold, but you think you are. Does it matter?"

"It does matter, because I am cold. That's what makes me so good at what I do. You need to know the type of man you're proclaiming your love for."

"Would you stop saying that. I do know!"

"You don't know shit! Do you know that I shot you and tried to kill you? You lived, but the baby you were carrying, Supreme's baby, who was supposed to be your first born child, died, because of me."

"You're lying."

"No, I'm not. So, again, nah, I ain't mourning over trife trash, like Tori. 'Cause as much as I loved you, when you crossed me, I was ready for you to die, so you know I ain't losing no sleep over a parasite like Tori."

"What did I do that was so horrible you wanted me dead?"

"You stole money from me, fucked my best friend, and set me up to spend the rest of my life in prison. All because you found out I cheated on you wit' some bum chick that I didn't give a fuck about."

"I see. We must've forgiven one another, because we share a daughter together."

"We did. But the point is..."

"There is no point," I said, interrupting Nico. "We can stand here and rehash the past, because I'm sure we've both done a lot of horrible things to each other, or we can focus on now. I don't have blinders on. I know you're flawed, so am I. It doesn't matter though, because I need you and you need me, too."

"You're right, I do need you, but I want you to

fully comprehend what comes with me…with us."

"I do. It's called unconditional love."

I held Nico and if I had my way, I would never let him go. Through a tragedy we found our way back to each other and I loved him now more than ever.

Aaliyah

"I wasn't expecting to see you today," I said, letting Amir in.

"I came over to invite you to my birthday party."

"You could've called. It's okay to admit you're checking up on me. By the way, I saw your hired help patrolling the outside of my building."

"Somebody needs to watch over you."

"Well, you can take them off duty. I'm headed to Miami."

"Is that right."

"Yep. I need to get back to business and I miss my boyfriend, but I won't be gone that long. When is your birthday party?"

"Next Saturday."

"Good, I'll be back in time."

"Here's your invite," Amir said, handing me a black and gold tri-fold invitation.

"Impressive." The outside was covered with black silk and crystals, with gold embroidery. The inside was drenched in gold, with a black foil monogram at the top and beautiful swirl and crest details. A stunning crystal buckle adorned the back, for added elegance.

"Latreese designed it. She thought I should go all out and have a huge birthday bash, very upscale."

"I'm looking forward to attending. It's always fun to have an excuse to dress up in fab clothes."

"There's something else I also wanted to talk to you about."

"Come back to my bedroom and tell me while I'm packing. So, what's up?" I said unzipping my roller bag.

"It's regarding the tap on Emory's phone."

"He didn't find out about that, did he?"

"No."

"Then what...you're not still tapping his phone, are you?" Amir stood silent with a stupid look on his face. "Why would you keep tapping his phone?

After he was cleared in my mother's shooting that was supposed to be the end of it. I don't like Emory, but everybody deserves some privacy."

"I kept it going a little longer. I wanted to make sure we didn't miss anything."

"You full of shit liar. You kept tabs on Emory for your own self-gain. That's pretty foul."

"I think it's foul Emory is cutting side deals and not including you, or his brother." I stopped folding the jeans I was about to put in my luggage and stared at Amir.

"Side deals?"

"Yes. Seems that the millions you all are bringing in aren't enough for him. You want to be partners with somebody like that?"

"I've never trusted Emory. Our relationship isn't based on trust, it's about money."

"Yeah, some of the money he's conveniently keeping to himself."

"Amir, this doesn't change the fact that you're continuing to listen to his phones calls."

"I've already shut it down. We're done listening to Emory's calls, but I thought you should know what he was up to."

"If you're expecting a thank you from me, forget it."

"So, you're mad, I get it. I hope you'll be over it by next weekend."

"I'm still coming to your stupid party," I said, tossing a pillow at Amir's head.

"Aaliyah, are you here?" I heard my mom calling out.

"Yes, here I come. Aren't I popular today," I said, going out in the hallway to see my mother. "This is a pleasant surprise," I smiled, hugging my mom. "What brings you to the city?"

"I just wanted to spend some time with my baby girl. Amir, I didn't know you were here."

"I was about to leave. I came to drop off Aaliyah's invitation to my birthday party. I hope you and Nico are coming."

"Yes, we will be there."

"Good. Aaliyah, you have a safe trip. I'll talk to you when you get back."

"Okay, I'll call you...bye."

"I had no idea you were going out of town. Where you headed?"

"Miami. Come on, let's sit down. I can finish

packing later. I have some time before I need to leave to catch my flight."

"You're off to see your boyfriend, the one I haven't met yet."

"Since you got out of the hospital, it's been nonstop drama. Meeting Dale isn't a priority, you getting better is."

"I am better. I've been better for weeks now."

"Are you starting to remember anything new, about us, our family?"

"No, but your father has been cluing me in."

"What has he told you?"

"He told me about the time he shot me and I almost died, losing the baby I was having with Supreme."

"Daddy shot you?"

"Oh gosh, I figured you knew, Aaliyah. It was so many years ago, before you were even born. I'm sorry," my mom said, putting her hand over her mouth, as if wishing she could take back what she said.

"That must've been what Supreme was talking about, after you got shot and he said he had been through this before. My family is something else," I sulked. I stood up, so I could go to the kitchen. I had to pour myself a glass of wine. "I need a drink. Can I get you one, too?"

"Sure. Aaliyah, I didn't mean to upset you," I heard my mom say, while I was reaching for the wine glasses. That was the last thing I was expecting my mother to tell me. Some secrets were better left untold.

"How do you feel about rekindling your relationship with Nico, after finding that out?" I asked, handing my mother her wine.

"It doesn't change my feelings. We've become even closer."

"I'm not even going to pretend to understand that type of love."

"Is that a photo album?" my mom questioned, reaching on the table to pick it up.

"Yeah. I was going through it the other day."

"These are pictures of my wedding to Supreme."

"Aren't they beautiful? You were a gorgeous bride and you still look exactly the same. How crazy is that."

"I seem so happy in these pictures."

"You always looked happy when you were with Supreme. You all did have some tough times, but the love was undeniable, and when you were pregnant with Xavier, daddy gave you the world. He went out of his way to spoil me, too, because he didn't want me to feel left out. He is such an amazing man and father."

"I know this must be hard for you. Seeing all these pictures with us as a family, we were happy."

"I would give anything for you to remember. These are some of the best memories of my life and I should be sharing them with you."

"I know, but I'm alive and here with you, now. Maybe I'll get my memory back, maybe I won't, but it won't change the love I have for you and Xavier. Your little brother is so special. I'm grateful to be blessed with two incredible kids."

I put my head down as sorrow swept over me. I didn't want to let go of the mother I knew before, but in a lot of ways she was gone. This was a new Precious Cummings, and I had to start accepting that.

"You're right. I have you now and I love you, so much," I said, hugging my mother.

"I love you, too. Now, I'ma let you get back to packing, so you can catch your flight. I want to meet this boyfriend of yours very soon."

"You will...I promise. Where are you off to, now?

Are you going to do some shopping while you're in the city?"

"No, I'm having dinner with your grandfather and Maya."

"Maya, ahhh, don't make me vomit."

"Be nice," my mom laughed.

"Besides, you and Supreme getting back together, if I could have one wish come true, it would be you remembering how much you detest your sister."

"If I can forgive Nico for shooting me and killing my unborn child, then I think I should at least attempt to make amends with my sister."

"When you put it like that, you have a valid point, but be careful. I'm not convinced Maya can be rehabilitated."

"I'll keep both eyes open. I love you." My mother gave me a kiss on the cheek. "Call me when you get to Miami."

"Will do."

I loathed Maya, but for my mother's sake, I wanted her to change. It was apparent my mother had every intention on building a relationship with her sister and with all she had been through,

I wanted it to work; but if Maya hurt my mother one more time, I would make it my business to personally blow her brains out.

Precious

I had so much on my mind, as I strolled through the lobby, exiting the apartment building. Instead of looking ahead, I was focused on the marble floor, lost in my thoughts. It wasn't until I bumped into someone, that I started paying attention.

"I apologize," I said to a teenage girl, who was on her iPhone. She graciously smiled and waved me off.

"Precious, how are you?" it took me a few seconds to zero in on the well-dressed man, but once I did, I instantly recognized him.

"I'm good. How are you, Supreme?"

"Maintaining."

"I guess you're here to see Aaliyah."

"Yes. She told me you were doing very well. You certainly look the part." I glanced down at my blue knit Alexander McQueen crop top and matching pencil skirt, teamed with some studded Jimmy Choo pumps, as if I didn't remember what I walked out the house wearing.

"Thank you."

"How are things progressing with you and Nico?"

Supreme questioning me about Nico caught me off guard. "Are you sure you want to know?"

"I wouldn't have asked if I didn't."

"We're in a good place."

"With everything Nico put us through, he's the one you remember loving. The irony in that."

"He told me some of the things that happened and in the past."

"Did he tell you about our baby?"

"Yes, he did."

"But yet you stay with him. Why am I surprised? You forgave Nico before, why wouldn't you forgive him again. Maybe the two of you really are meant for each other."

"Do I hear cynicism in your voice?"

"Maybe you do. I would've rather you woke up remembering being in love with Lorenzo, than Nico. There is no love lost between us."

"I had no control over who I woke up loving."

"I know this. What makes it so hard is that you almost lost your life trying to save mine. You must've truly loved me, even more than I realized. But that no longer matters, because you don't love me anymore."

I watched as Supreme headed to the elevator and I remained frozen in my tracks for a few minutes. He was the man I almost died for and he meant nothing to me now. I couldn't shed a tear for Supreme, even if I wanted to.

"There's my girl," Quentin said, greeting me when I sat down at the table.

"Precious, you look beautiful."

"Thank you, Maya. You look beautiful, too."

"My two daughters complimenting each other; this dinner is off to a good start."

"I told you I wanted to give this a try and I

meant it."

"I'm sure everybody has warned you to stay away from me, so I appreciate you trying. I will admit we have a very rocky history and most of it is all my fault, but I have changed." Quentin squeezed Maya's hand, as if confirming her words were the truth.

"From what I can gather, a lot of people made mistakes, including me. I'm on a forgiveness tour and you, Maya, are one of the stops. Unfortunately, there are other people I can't make things right with."

"Are you speaking of Supreme?" Quentin asked.

"Yes. I ran into him after visiting Aaliyah. I can't understand how a man that I loved so much, I now feel absolutely nothing for."

"I always thought Supreme was your soulmate and that the two of you would find your way back to each other, no matter what. This goes to show you really don't have control over your destiny."

"I hate to leave right when things were getting good, but can you ladies excuse me for a moment? I see an associate of mine over at that table I need to speak to. I'll be back shortly."

"Who doesn't daddy know? Everywhere we go, he has to stop and talk to somebody."

"From what I've noticed, Quentin is definitely a people person."

"He is and I think people love him so much, because he tries to see the best in everybody."

"Especially his kids."

"I guess you're referring to me."

"It's no secret that everybody in my life has warned me to stay away from you. No one has had one decent word to say on your behalf, except for Quentin."

"That's because our father has taken the time to get to understand me. He knows what I've been through and that I've changed."

"Have you really changed or is it all smoke and mirrors? Having Quentin on your side puts you in an excellent position. He yields a lot of power and influence. I would hate for you to be taking advantage of him."

"Precious, I promise that I'm not. Like I said before, I made a ton of mistakes and there was a period in my life I wasn't a good person, but that's all changed. Finally meeting my father and having somebody in my life that genuinely loves me unconditionally has made me want to be a better person. I just hope you give me a chance, so you can see for yourself."

"I want to believe you, not only for our father's sake, but for my own."

Maya reached her hand across the table and placed it on top of mine. "We're sisters. That's a special bond and we shouldn't let anyone come between it."

"If you are who you claim to be and the change has been made, then no one will be able to come between us. For your sake, you better be telling the truth."

Aaliyah

Being in Miami, if only for a few days, was exactly what I needed to rejuvenate. Lying by the mosaic infinity pool, with underwater seating, this new home Dale bought was definitely the Crown Jewel of Sunset Island. The sun cascaded down on my body, taking my mind to a peaceful place.

"I could stand here and stare at you all day," Dale said, lusting after me. But I couldn't blame him. With my skin glistening in this black floral print Fendi monokini, I was ready to lust after myself.

"No need to stare, you can touch...it's all yours," I teased, and then took a sip of my mango daiquiri.

"Don't tempt me. I would love to slip you out

of that bathing suit right now."

"So, what's stopping you?" I asked, tilting down my sunglasses so I could make direct eye contact with Dale.

"The front gate called to let me know we're having company."

"Who? I thought since I was only going to be here for a few days, we were going to relax and just enjoy each other's company."

"And we are, but Emory needed to come over and speak to us about some things. He said it wouldn't take long."

"Leave it up to your brother to interrupt my mini vacay."

"You said yourself you also came to handle some business."

"True, but I thought I would be able to handle it with you. I didn't think I needed to see Emory in order to do so."

"Play nice…for me," Dale said, giving me a kiss. "I promise I'm gonna make sure the next couple of days are perfect."

"If you put it like that, I guess I can be nice to Emory. Plus, I do owe you. You were so understanding about me accusing you and your brother of putting that hit on my family. Especially, since I turned out to be wrong."

"To be honest with you, I was more hurt than angry. I want you to trust me." Before I could respond to Dale, we saw Emory walking up.

"What up brother," Emory said, as the brothers knocked fist. "Aaliyah, good to see you. How's your family?"

"Everything is coming along," I smiled.

"Glad to hear."

"So, what did you need to speak to us about?"

"I might have a new heroin connect. The prices are excellent. I think we should make a switch and start fuckin' with them instead. Of course, we're partners, so I need for us to agree on it."

"The new connect can give us better prices than we're getting now?"

"That's right."

"I don't care how excellent their prices are. Alvarez has the best quality heroin around...period. Why would we stop fuckin' wit' him for your new people?" I spit.

"You don't even know the quality of my new

connects heroin. Customers love it just as much, if not more than, Alvarez's product."

"How would you know, unless you've already been doing business with this so-called new connect."

"Now you reaching, Aaliyah. Of course I had some fiends sample it, so I could get feedback, but I haven't started doing business with the new connect yet."

"Lies you tell."

"Aaliyah, I thought we had an understanding," Dale said, eyeing me.

"It's hard to be nice to somebody, when you know they are telling you bold faced lies."

"What the hell is you talkin' 'bout now? First, you accuse me and my brother of putting that hit on your family, now you saying I'm dealing with another connect behind your back. When does the madness stop?"

"First of all, I had every right to think you had something to do with the shooting, 'cause that's what the fuck Tori told me. So, she lied, but that's not my motherfuckin' problem. When I found out the truth, I apologized to Dale, now we can move the fuck on."

"You didn't apologize to me."

"Why the fuck would I? You're the one who introduced me to Tori, and you're the one that she pointed the finger at. If anybody owe you an apology, it's her, but since she's dead that ain't gon' happen."

"Both of you chill. We supposed to be discussing business, not listening to the two of you argue over bullshit."

"Maybe you need to explain that to yo' lil' girlfriend."

"I ain't nobody's lil' nothin', motherfucker. The fact is, Dale, your brother is cutting side deals behind our backs. Emory, you can deny the shit all you want to."

"Are you sure?"

"Yo, I know you don't believe this broad!" Emory belted.

Dale stood between Emory and me. He stared at me, then back at his brother. Emory was breathing extra hard, like he was amped. It almost appeared like he wanted to swing at me and I knew the nigga was a liar, but Emory damn sure wasn't stupid, and he wanted to live.

"You keep playin' crazy wit' me, I'ma fuck around and give yo' brother names of who you cutting them side deals wit'. 'Cause see me personally, I don't even give a fuck. I wasn't even gon' say shit. I never trusted yo' ass and I expect you to cut side deals. As long as I'm making a certain amount of money, you can cut all the side deals you want. Now, you crossing your brother, well, that's another Bronx Tale. But what I'm not gon' do is let you stand in front of me and act like all yo' shit is sweet, and co-sign on you cutting our business relationship off with Mr. Alvarez. Nah motherfucker, that, I won't do."

"Fine, we don't have to stop doing business with Mr. Alvarez."

"I bet you we don't," I said taking another sip of my drink. I could tell from Dale's body stance that he was pissed. He knew deep down I was telling the truth and the shit was fuckin' with him.

"My business here is done. I'll call you later, Dale," Emory said, before walking away. Dale sat in the lounge chair next to me and kept his head down for a few minutes, without saying a word.

"How do you know my brother is cutting side deals? I want the truth, Aaliyah."

"I had his phone tapped," I admitted, without hesitation.

Dale shook his head. "I'm assuming this was during the time you were trying to find out if we had anything to do with the shooting?"

"Exactly. Tapping his phone cleared both of you, regarding the shooting, but it implicated Emory in that other bullshit he doing. And again, I wasn't surprised. Your brother is shady and you know that shit, too."

"I do, but I didn't think he would be shady with me. You really weren't gon' tell me?"

"I was debating it, but a part of me really didn't care. I do understand why you would care, so a part of me did want to tell you, but I also didn't want you or Emory to know that I had been listening to his private conversations."

"Yo, this is really fucked up. I can't even trust my own brother."

"At least now you know to watch his ass."

"But damn, I didn't want to have to watch my brother. This game can bring out the worst in people, for sure. I don't want that to be me. I appreciate you telling me the truth, though."

"I suggest you tell Emory to change his numbers, though, because although the person who was tapping his phone said they stopped, I don't believe it. At this point, I think we know enough and everybody deserves some privacy, including Emory."

"You're right. I need to figure out how to handle him, though. I want to make sure whatever side business my brother got going doesn't interfere with our business. That shit could easily turn messy."

"I didn't think about that, but you're right."

"I like hearing you say that."

"Say what?"

"That I'm right."

"Oh, shut up," I giggled, hitting Dale in his arm.

"Now, only if I can get you to admit that I'm right about it being time to meet your family."

"First, I needed to prove that you weren't the enemy. I couldn't have you meeting my family, only for them to kill you."

"True, but we're past that, now."

"No doubt. I have an idea. Amir is having this big fancy birthday party this Saturday. You should come as my date. All my family will be there and it will be fun, so everybody will be in a good mood, so no pressure. What do you say?"

"What do I need to wear?" Dale smiled, giving me a kiss. He slipped me out of my bathing suit and next thing I knew, we were both floating in the pool, naked.

Precious

"Are you sure you're up to going to this party tonight?"

"Of course I am. I need to dress up, go out, and have a good time. Even at my last doctor visit, he recommended as long as I was up to it, I should get back to my regular routine."

"As long as you're up to it, I won't fight you."

"Good, because the skintight, metallic, Armani Prive gown I bought to wear is gorgeous. You're going to love to see me in it and you're going to love taking it off of me even more."

"Really," Nico said, lifting up my hair and kissing my neck. "Maybe we should skip the party and stay here. Everything I need is right here in this room."

"Patience, my love. Now, let me go get dressed, before you change my mind."

As I headed upstairs, out of nowhere, this excruciating pain shot through my head. I grabbed onto the staircase, so I wouldn't lose my balance. I glanced behind me, to make sure Nico didn't see what happened. If he thought for one moment something was wrong with me, the only place I would be going was to the emergency room.

When I got to the master bathroom, I took two pain killer pills that my doctor had given me. I hadn't needed to take them in weeks, but tonight was different. I turned the knob to take a hot shower, not wanting to dwell on the discomfort. I felt myself dozing in and out, so I sat down on the glass bench, inside the shower, letting the water rain down on me. Within a few minutes, my mind had completely gone someplace else.

Flashes of faces, places, and things kept flipping through my head, but I didn't recognize any of it. I seemed to be traveling back in the past. *Who are these people and where am I?* I asked myself over and over again, until in an instant I snapped out of my daze and was back to present.

"What the hell is going on with me? Could I be trying to get my memory back or am I hallucinating?" I asked myself the questions out loud, as if I expected someone to miraculously give me the answers.

"Precious, are you okay in there?" I heard Nico call out.

"I'm fine," I lied, as I got my bearings together. "I'll be out shortly.

I refused to let a headache, flashbacks, or anything else ruin my night. I stepped under the showerhead, closed my eyes, and fixated on the amazing night Nico and I would share together.

"Amir went all out for his birthday," Nico commented, when we stepped into the venue, on the Upper East Side.

"He must have spent a pretty penny," I added, observing the elaborate design. The space wasn't large, it was well suited for an intimate party, but it screamed money. The floor-to-ceiling windows offered gorgeous views of the park on one side and a panoramic view of the New York Skyline, including the Statue of Liberty, on the other. There was Art Deco style furnishings, marble floors, Corinthian style columns, and 7-story vaulted ceilings, with enormous sheer curtains hanging from them. The elegance was on a staggering scale.

"Mommy! So glad you came. You look unbelievable."

"Thank you, but look at you. That dress is to die for."

"Isn't it daring," Aaliyah grinned, doing a quick spin around, so I could get a good look at her couture black gown, with see-through panels.

"Yes, it is. So daring, I'm tempted to take off my tuxedo jacket and make you put it on."

"Daddy, be quiet. It isn't that risqué; plus, I have my man here to watch over me."

"You brought Dale?" I asked, with my eyes widening in anticipation, at the thought of meeting Aaliyah's boyfriend.

"Yes, he's coming this way, now." I looked over in the direction Aaliyah was staring.

"Aaliyah, he is beyond handsome. He looks like a young version of..."

"Of who, mom?"

"I don't know. I'm just rambling. Looks wise, he's a keeper."

"Glad that you approve."

"I'm glad your mother is impressed, but it's going to take more than looks to get my approval," Nico said, eyeing Dale as he approached.

"Dale, these are my parents."

"It's a pleasure to meet you both." Dale extended his hand to Nico, and then me. I smiled, pleasantly pleased with his easygoing demeanor. Nico, on the other hand, was wearing his best screw face.

"I have been anxiously waiting for Aaliyah to introduce you to us. I had to meet the man who was special enough to capture my daughter's heart."

"Mother, would you stop. You're embarrassing me."

"So, you're saying I haven't captured your heart?" Dale inquired in a teasing way to Aaliyah. I noticed he had this charming grin that highlighted his right dimple. If Aaliyah weren't already in love with the charismatic man, soon she would be.

"I'm not having this conversation here with you, especially not in front of my parents."

"I have no reservations about expressing my feelings for your daughter. I don't know if I've captured her heart, but she has most definitely captured mine."

From the expression on Aaliyah's face, she was taken aback by Dale's declaration. It tickled my heart to see my daughter blushing. She was wearing love well.

"Dale, I don't know you and from what I do know, I'm a bit apprehensive about your relationship with my daughter; but Aaliyah is grown, and I believe smart enough to make her own decisions. Do take this as a warning though: if my daughter ever comes to me saying you've mistreated her in any way, you will be dealt with. Now, excuse me, I need to go speak to Genesis."

"Please, excuse her father. Aaliyah is his only child, so he can be overbearing sometimes, when it comes to her."

"No need to explain. When I have a daughter, I'll be the same way. Aaliyah is a very special woman and her father has every right to want to protect her."

"Dale, would you go get me a drink, please?"

“Sure, would you like something, too?” he asked.

“No, I’m good, but thanks. Aaliyah, he is a keeper,” I said, once he had walked off.

“He’s not going to want to stay around much longer, if daddy keeps making threats like he just did.”

“Don’t pay your father any mind. Dale handled it perfectly. I think he knows how to deal with Nico. I really do like Dale, though. I get good vibes from him.”

“I have to admit, I’m pretty crazy about him, myself. He makes me happy.”

“I’m glad, because you deserve it. There’s nothing like love in the air.”

“Speaking of which, is that Genesis with a date?” Aaliyah nodded her head in his direction. He was still talking to Nico, and there was a woman standing beside him rather closely. “I have never seen Genesis with a woman before. Is that his date?”

“I am getting date from their body language. Is it me or does she look very familiar.”

“You’re right. She has her hair down and she’s all dolled up, but that’s the Skylar chick from L.A. I knew they were crushing on each other.”

"So did I, but I thought Genesis agreed that he did not need to go there with her."

"Clearly, he's changed his mind and that black and gold one shoulder gown she has on is Emilio Puccini. I know this because I was going to buy it for the party, but got this dress instead. I don't know Miss Skylar's job credentials, but I seriously doubt she can afford a dress like that. That means Genesis had to foot the bill. Let me find out Amir's father is seriously checkin' for this chick."

I listened to every word coming out of Aaliyah's mouth and I was afraid that was exactly what was going on. "This isn't good," I said, under my breath. I was on my way to have a word with Genesis, when Quentin and Maya approached.

"I'm a lucky man. The three most beautiful women at this party are surrounding me."

"Grandfather, you're so silly." Aaliyah and I both gave him a hug. When Maya reached over to also hug us, I reciprocated, but Aaliyah leaned back, as if her aunt was contagious. I didn't say anything, because Aaliyah accepting Maya would have to be of her own free will.

"Would you all excuse me? I need to have a

word with Nico."

"Go ahead. We'll be right here. My daughter and granddaughter need to get better acquainted, anyway."

"Good luck with that," I winked and headed towards my real target, Genesis. By this time, Nico had moved on talking to some other acquaintances and Genesis was engrossed in a conversation with Skylar. I couldn't lie: homegirl was wearing the hell out of that dress. When I first met her, she was a very pretty girl in a plain Jane way, but all done up, Skylar was undeniably stunning. And she was definitely Genesis's type, because he loved him some chocolate girls.

"Hello," Genesis said, when I walked up.

"Precious, you look beautiful," Skylar stated, giving me a warm smile.

"Thank you, and you look quite beautiful, yourself. That dress is everything and you're wearing it perfectly.

"That's so sweet of you to say. Genesis picked it out."

"Genesis always had great taste. Skylar, do you mind if I speak to him for a moment? It's regarding business."

"No problem. I need to use the restroom anyway. I'll be back," she smiled at Genesis.

"Before you start..."

"Don't even try to justify this," I said, before Genesis could even continue. "I thought we agreed that Skylar was not a good fit for you."

"It's just a party, Precious."

"Oh, please. Aaliyah stated to me that she has never seen you with a woman and Nico said you're a workaholic and never date. So, don't try to act like flying this woman in, buying her an expensive designer dress, and bringing her to your son's private birthday party is no big deal."

"I know how to set boundaries. I'm enjoying Skylar's company, nothing more, nothing less."

"Lie to yourself if you want, but don't lie to Skylar."

"I'm not lying to her."

"Pretending that the two of you can have a real relationship is lying to her. You're the head of one of the biggest drug operations on the east coast. Your life is constantly in danger and so is anybody around you. Does Skylar know that?"

"Here she comes. Lets finish this conversation

later."

"Did I come back too soon?" Skylar beamed, in her sweet girl-next-door voice.

"No, we're done."

"Precious, I'm going to be here for a few more days. Besides Genesis, I don't know anybody in New York. I would love if we could have lunch or dinner while I'm here."

"I think that would be great. Don't you, Genesis?"

"Yes, I do. If anybody knows New York, it's Precious Cummings."

"Skylar, get my number from Genesis and we'll set something up."

"Thanks, I'll give you a call tomorrow."

Genesis seemed happy with Skylar and they did make a cute couple. Unfortunately, my gut told me nothing good would come of it. I knew Genesis would survive it, wasn't so sure Skylar could endure it.

Aaliyah

I practically spit out my drink when I caught Latreese parading in the party, like she was the lady of the hour. She was draped on Amir's arm, like a cheap fur coat, and had the audacity to have her nose tilted all the way up in the air. The two of them made a beeline directly over to us and I put on my fakest smile.

"Hey, birthday boy! Happy Birthday to you, Amir." I gave Amir a harmless, friendly kiss on the cheek, but I caught Latreese rolling her eyes at me. I played it off like I didn't see her, to keep the peace. "Dale, this is the man of the hour and my dear childhood friend, Amir."

"Nice to meet you," Dale said, shaking Amir's

hand.

"And I'm Amir's girlfriend, Latreese," she said extending her hand, which Dale politely took.

"Your event planner did a fabulous job with this party. I mean, it is Hollywood red carpet all the way."

"Thank you."

"Oh, Latreese, you're an event planner? I had no idea. I thought Leslie's company put this together."

"No, I'm not, but I played a pivotal role with helping the event planner put this party together."

"You all did an excellent job."

"Thanks. If I knew you were in town I would've had them hire you as one of our bartenders. That is what you do back in Miami, right...pour drinks?"

Is this heffa trying to play me right now? Do I pour drinks? How about I pour the rest of my drink right in your face? Where does Amir find these stray animals? I thought to myself, as I kept my cool.

"I have dabbled in bartending and a few other odd jobs. You have the luxury of doing that when you're a trust fund baby, like myself." Dale shook his head and laughed at my remark. Amir didn't appear to be as amused.

"Amir, can I borrow you for a minute," Leslie, the party planner said.

"Sure."

"I'll be right here waiting for you," Latreese said, batting her eyes.

"Babe, I need to take this call. I'll be right back."

"I guess that just leaves us," Latreese quipped.

"I guess so. Hopefully both our dates will be back soon."

"Dates?" Latreese glared. "I'm beyond dating Amir. We're a couple. Don't you see this Neil Lane diamond necklace he got me? And this isn't the Kay Jewelers collection, either. He got this from Cartier."

"Does that mean it's on loan and has to be returned tomorrow?"

"No, it doesn't. It was a gift."

"Calm down. No need to get offensive."

"What is your issue with me? Are you jealous because Amir is with me and not you?"

"First of all, I'm the one that left New York, which meant me leaving Amir."

"I know and I'm still trying to understand why you came back. Is it because of Amir?"

"My family is here and I came back for them, not Amir. Although I'm sure you would like me to be, but there is nothing you have that I'm jealous of and that includes Amir."

"You think you are such hot shit."

"Yeah, I do and your point."

"Just watch yourself."

"Hold up," I laughed, waving my hand in delight. "You can't possibly be threatening me," I laughed some more.

"Take it however you want to take it."

"I was giggling and shit wit' you 'cause I found you humorous, but I wasn't laughing with you, I was laughing at you. Let me explain one thing. I might kee kee with you, but you don't ever want it with me. Tricks like you come up missing. Check my stats. Now, let me excuse myself before I really say something that will make you scared to leave your crib ever again."

"Where are you going?" Amir grabbed my arm and asked, as I was headed in the opposite direction of his girlfriend.

"I need another drink."

"Did it get that bad between you and Latreese?"

"Everything went fine."

"You don't have to lie to me, Aaliyah. I know you all don't really care for each other, but it would mean a lot to me if you gave Latreese a chance."

"I don't need any new friends. You see what sort of hell Justina put me through and we were childhood friends. Speaking of Justina, I'm surprised she's not here or could she not handle your relationship with Latreese?"

"Justina has accepted I've moved on. She was actually supposed to come, but I just spoke to her father and he said she missed her flight, and won't be here until tomorrow."

"T-Roc is here?"

"Yep. You know he's one of my dad's closest friends."

"That's right. I just hadn't heard his name mentioned in awhile. Does he still have Chantal locked away in a crazy house, so she doesn't have to go to jail?"

"I thought you knew."

"Knew what?"

"Chantal's attorney copped her a plea deal. She had to do two years in a psychiatric facility, continue to get therapy once she's released, and 10 years probation. Justina told me her mother should be getting out within the next few months."

"My life was turned upside down and I spent almost a year in jail, because of that mother and daughter deadly duo, and Chantal gets a slap on the wrist. And Justina never was held accountable for all her lies. Must be nice."

"What happened to you was wrong, but Justina has a lot of issues she had to deal with, and is still dealing with."

"You never learn. You always feel sorry for these kooky women. Now, you're with a girl that's as crazy, if not crazier than Justina, and you don't even see it."

"Latreese is not crazy."

"So says the man that keeps a crazy woman by his side. I wish you good luck, but trust you'll eventually see that I'm right. Speaking of kooky women, who is that man Maya is talking to?" Amir turned to see who I was talking about.

"I don't know."

"So, he wasn't on your guest list."

"Nope, but it doesn't mean he didn't come as

somebody else's guest."

"His interaction with Maya seems a tad off to me. You see like they're talking...like they want to make sure nobody can hear what they're saying."

"Aaliyah, you over analyze everything. You've labeled Latreese crazy and now Maya is conspiring with a guest at my birthday party. You should relax. Go, get your drink and enjoy the party. I need to get back to Latreese."

Nine times out of ten, my instincts were never wrong and I heard alarms going off. When I saw Maya and the mystery man sneaking out, I decided to follow them. Luckily, the venue was crowded, so neither of them noticed I was on their trail. They were outside, standing in front of a black truck, enthralled in a conversation, but I couldn't hear a word of what they were saying. I wanted to move closer, but feared I would be seen, so I had to stay put.

Their conversation continued for another fifteen minutes, sometimes becoming heated. For a second, I wondered if they were having a lovers quarrel, but I wasn't picking up any romantic vibes. As their relationship seemed to be winding down, Maya playfully hit the man on his upper arm and I noticed him flinch, then rubbing the area she hit.

Could that be the motherfucker that ran up in my crib trying to get at me? I don't know where, but I did shoot him because I saw the blood. Could he be rubbing the spot he took the bullet? Is Maya behind the man trying to kidnap me? Oh hell, nah! I have to get to the bottom of this shit, because if Maya is up to her old tricks, that ho gon' have to be put down, I thought to myself.

Precious

"You look absolutely beautiful tonight." I heard someone say to me, when I came out of the restroom. I looked to see the face that went with the voice and a very tall, extremely handsome, well-dressed man was standing in front of me.

"Do I know you?"

"I guess it is true, you lost your memory, but the important thing is you're alive."

"Will you please tell me who you are?"

"Lorenzo."

"I was in love with you."

"You do remember me?"

"No, that came out wrong. Several people have told me that before the accident, I was in love with

you."

"Yes, we were in love with each other."

"I apologize, I don't remember, but I must say, I have incredible taste in men: Nico, Supreme, and now you. I'm impressed with myself."

"I see losing your memory hasn't had a negative affect on your sense of humor."

"No, it hasn't. Although I don't remember what we shared, I'm glad I was able to finally meet you. I had heard your name so many times, but now I have a face to go with the name."

"Yes, you do, but I'm not giving up hope."

"Hope on what, that I'll remember?"

"Yes," Lorenzo nodded. "You came into my life and changed it for the better. I'll always love you for that."

"What the fuck is going on over here?"

"Nico. I ran into Lorenzo and we were talking."

"You don't even remember him, so why are ya'll talking?"

"Nico, chill. I saw Precious coming out the bathroom and we started having a conversation."

"You mean you initiated a conversation," Nico barked.

"No need to be hostile, my man."

"Nico, why are you acting like this?"

"You don't know this dude."

"I thought he was one of your business partners."

"On paper only. The relationship stops there. It's strictly business."

"I thought we were past this. You finally get the girl and you still don't know how to act. Is it because you won by default and you're feeling slightly insecure?"

"Fuck you, Lorenzo!" Nico roared, jumping towards Lorenzo, ready to come to blows.

"Nico, stop! That's enough." Fortunately, Genesis, Amir, and a few other men were in close enough proximity to keep Nico and Lorenzo apart, before a fight broke out.

"Precious is with me now. Remember that shit and respect it. She don't know who you are, so stay the fuck away. Business partners or not, I'll fuck you up."

Lorenzo put his hands up as if calling for peace, before saying, "I understand you only won back the love of your life because she doesn't remember anybody else. That would shake my confidence, too, so I'm going to excuse your outburst. You a lil' sensitive right now…I get it.'"

"Fuck you, Lorenzo!" Nico spit again, as Genesis escorted Lorenzo away from the drama.

"Everything is fine. Everybody go back to what you were doing and enjoy the party. There's nothing to see here," Amir stated, trying to diffuse the commotion.

"I think we should go. You're upset and you'll be in a bad mood for the rest of the night."

"I'm fine."

"No, you're not."

"Are we good over here?" Genesis asked, coming back to check on Nico.

"No," I replied.

"Yes, we are," Nico countered.

"Which one is it?"

"Man, I'm over this shit. Just make sure Lorenzo stays away from Precious, and we're good."

"Nico, I'm ready to go. Genesis, give our apologies to Amir."

"That won't be necessary. We're family, things happen. Nico, I'll call you tomorrow."

On our drive home, I replayed the bullshit that went down at Amir's birthday party. An evening that was supposed to solidify me being back on the scene and feeling better than ever turned into a night I would prefer to forget. I remember Nico being the territorial type, but his level of hatred and what I chalked up as jealousy towards Lorenzo, had me stumped. Had I really been that in love with Lorenzo, that it was still an intimidating factor for Nico? I didn't want it to be like this. I was more in love with him than ever before. I had to figure out a way to make Nico feel secure in our relationship and know that I wasn't going anywhere.

"Thanks so much for meeting up with me, Precious. Especially since it was so last minute," Skylar beamed, when I sat down across from her at the restaurant.

"My pleasure. I was already in the city visiting my sister, so when you called it was perfect timing.

"Luck was on my side, because I didn't want to leave New York, without spending some time with

you."

"Don't take this the wrong way, but why was that so important to you? I mean, it's not like we're friends."

"I want us to be."

"Skylar, I really don't have room in my life for new friends, I barely remember my old ones. I'm not sure if you're aware of this, but not that long ago, I was shot, almost died, and lost my memory."

"Genesis did mention it to me. It's understandable you would be reluctant to bring new people into your circle, but because you have a close relationship with him and our relationship is getting serious, I thought maybe you would reconsider."

"How is your relationship getting serious? The two of you barely know each other."

"If you're going strictly by the number of days, then that would be true, but if you're basing it on how we connect, it's like we've known each other a lifetime."

I processed what Skylar said and I had to admit to myself that I got it. In a strange way, I felt the exact way about Genesis, but it wasn't in a romantic way. Although I lost my memory, when

Genesis came to the house to visit after I got out of the hospital, I instantly bonded with him and felt at ease. He possessed this energy that surrounded him and would draw you in.

"When you say serious, how serious?"

"I'm moving to New York with my son."

"If you don't mind me asking, what do you do for a living that you can move with your son, at the drop of a dime, from L.A. to New York?"

"Honestly, I'm a struggling model/actress. I do temp work on the side to pay the bills. I do have my bachelor's degree and worked as a paralegal for a year, before deciding to pursue my dreams. Having a baby put a minor hiccup in my plans, but my son has been a huge source of motivation."

"I see. Can't knock a woman for wanting to have it all. I assume you're going to continue and pursue your acting aspirations when you get to New York."

"Yes, and Genesis is behind me one hundred percent."

"Are you going to live with him?"

"Not initially. He's going to get us a place in the city. To make me feel secure about our arrangement, in case things don't work out between us, Genesis is going to put a substantial amount of money in a savings account for me. It's substantial for me, but probably a drop in the bucket for him. Regardless, it's very considerate."

"Yes, it is."

"That's why I'm hoping we can be friends. I'm moving to a new city and I can't be under Genesis all the time. Plus, there's something about you I like, Precious. When we were in L.A., initially, you were the only person who seemed to be looking out for me."

"Has Genesis told you what he does and what I do?"

"No, but I'm not stupid. I can put the pieces together."

"And it doesn't scare you?"

"I'm sure you weren't always in this life, did it scare you?"

"See, that's where you're wrong. This game chose me, but you, on the other hand, have a choice."

"No, I'm not scared. I believe Genesis will protect me and keep me out of harms way. He is the first man I've ever met that makes me feel like I can have it all: a career and a family, with an incredible man by my side. So, he's worth whatever risk I have to take."

"As long as you know what you're up against, then that's all that matters."

"I do and I appreciate you being upfront with me, and not trying to sell me a fairytale."

"As you get to know me, it will be evident that I don't do fairytales."

"Does that mean you're open for a potential friendship?"

"Why not. When I lost my memory, I said this would be an opportunity for new beginnings, so a new friendship might be exactly what I need."

"Great! Now, lets order some food, so we can eat, because I'm starving."

For the next couple hours, Skylar and I chatted like we were high school best friends playing catch up. The same way I got why she was crazy about Genesis, I got why he would be crazy about her, too. She was funny, candid, and extremely intelligent, but not in an irritating way. What was most appealing about Skylar was that she didn't take herself seriously. A lot of women would try to play the prima donna role, thinking it was cute and impressive, when actually it was a major turn off. But not Skylar, she meant what she said and said what she meant, and stood firm in her word. She was definitely winning me over.

"I really enjoyed our lunch," Skylar said, as we walked to my car.

"Me too. If I had one more drink, I would've had to call somebody and get a ride," I laughed.

"Lucky for me, I'm taking a cab, so I was able to have a few more extra glasses of wine."

"You don't have to take a cab. I can give you a ride. Are you staying with Genesis?"

"No, The Peninsula Hotel on Fifth Avenue and 55th Street."

"Get in, I'll take you."

"Are you sure?"

"Girl, of course, we're friends remember." We both giggled and got in the car. It wasn't until seatbelts were fastened and I was about to start the ignition that the masked gunman made his appearance known. He had been lurking in the backseat of the Range Rover and I didn't even know it. The dark tint made me not even notice.

"Start the car, do as I say, and maybe the both

of you will live to see another day."

I knew for a fact that once I drove off, Skylar and I were dead. Whoever this gunman was, he would have me drive us to a place where we would surly meet our doom. Without turning my head I observed Skylar. She was super quiet but her eyes were swelling with tears. Time was not my friend right now and I had to make my move quickly.

"You don't want to do this," I said, trying to stall as I figured out what the fuck to do.

"Shut up and move this car," the gunman said, matter-of-factly.

I was driving Nico's Range and I knew he kept a gun hidden right underneath his seat. You had to press a concealed button in order to get access. I argued with myself back and forth. Should I try my luck now and take the risk of being killed, or start the engine and try my luck in traffic. I said a silent prayer then without giving it a second thought made my move.

With my elbow I pressed the concealed button and with the arm that wasn't in the gunman's view I slowly retrieved the weapon. I wrapped my arm across my shoulder and blasted three shots without ever turning my head until after I heard his body slumping down in the seat. It all transpired so quickly that Skylar was shaking in her seat thinking the masked man still had his weapon aimed at us. It wasn't until I unlatched my seatbelt to get the gun out of the man's hand did it finally register to Skylar that he was dead.

"You killed him?" Skylar stuttered.

"Yes. Fuck!"

"What's wrong...is he still alive?" Skylar asked, sounding as if she was about to have a panic attack.

"No, he's dead, but I blew his face off, so I can't identify who he is and he doesn't have any identification on him," I sulked, pissed off.

"What are we going to do? We have a dead body in the car," Skylar stated, with her hands shaking hysterically.

I glanced over at Skylar, and then stared at her closely. Fear was holding her hostage. "I'm going to ask you again. Are you sure you're not scared? Because I don't think you're 'bout this life. You think about it while I place a phone call."

Skylar was in way over her head, but I already knew this. Maybe now that she got an up close and personal view of death knocking on her door for the second time, she would admit it to herself and stop fighting the truth. Because if she wanted to be Genesis's woman, not only would Skylar have to carry a weapon at all times, she would have to know how to pull the trigger, too.

Aaliyah

"Yo, what's the urgency? I figured you still be in the bed laid up under your man, the way you all looked so cozy at my party the other night."

"Dale had to catch a flight early this morning. He only came to attend your party with me. He had to get back to Miami, and handle some pending business."

"I see. So, what's up? On the phone you made it sound like this was an emergency."

"It is. I didn't have time to talk to you again before we left the party, but I'm telling you my instincts about Maya are dead on."

"You back to that shit again," Amir huffed, sitting down on the couch.

"Just hear me out. That mystery man she was enthralled in that conversation with."

"Man, they was probably talkin' 'bout fuckin' and when they could hook up."

"No. They took their conversation outside and I followed them. They were having a heated exchange until things seemed to simmer down."

"Okay...where's the big aha moment."

"Maya gave the guy a playful hit on his arm and he flinched like he was in pain. You know, the type of pain a bullet would cause."

"You think he's the man you shot when he ran up in your crib?"

"Yes. I'm telling you it's him. And if Maya is all buddy-buddy with him, that means they're working together."

"Are you sure you're right about this?"

"Positive, but there is only one way to find out. You need to put a tap on Maya's phone. Monitor her calls and see what the fuck she's up to."

"Give me all her info and I'll put my man on it. What if you're wrong and your paranoia is getting the best of you?"

"After you monitor her calls for a few weeks

and if you come up with nothing, you can stop. I'll admit I was wrong, but not a moment before."

"I'm on it, but get ready to admit you're wrong. Maya does love your grandfather and I think she genuinely wants a relationship with your mother. She doesn't want to fuck it up."

"Maybe you, my grandfather, and mother are all right about Maya, but I can't ignore the screaming noise coming from my gut."

"Maybe that noise you hear is the hatred you have for Maya consuming you."

"Whatever, you're salty at me because I told you your girlfriend is crazy. I'm right about her just like I'm right about Maya."

"How 'bout we agree not to discuss Latreese?"

"Fine with me. Hate to rush you off, but I'm on my way to Jersey to see my parents," I said taking Amir's hand, leading him to the front door. "Keep me posted on Maya and we'll talk later."

"Good afternoon beautiful, how are you?" I smiled, giving my mother a kiss when she opened the door.

"Better now that you're here. Come, let's sit outside by the pool."

"That's a wonderful idea. The weather is beautiful today."

"Yes. It isn't humid, nice breeze, perfect weather. Do you want Shelly to bring you out something to eat or drink?"

"No, I'm good, for now. Is dad here?" I asked, after getting comfortable in the armless lounge chair.

"No, he went to the city to handle some business with Genesis. So, it's just us girls."

"I prefer it that way," I joked. "Sitting out here is like being in heaven. I always forget how beautiful it is. It's like being on a resort, the garden, pool, then the lake, such a place of serenity."

"You're right. I find myself coming out here often. It's become like therapy for me."

"It everything okay with you? Are you and dad good?"

My mother let out a long, distressful sigh before answering. "Your father has been very distant with me since Amir's birthday party."

"Really? You all seemed so happy when I saw

you."

"I don't know where you disappeared to, but Nico and Lorenzo got into a huge altercation that was this close," my mother snapped her finger, "to turning into a full fledged fight. If it wasn't for Genesis, Amir, and some other guys stepping in and breaking things up, it would've been."

"Wow, I did miss that. It must've happened when I stepped out. Mom, I'm so sorry."

"Don't be sorry. I had no idea Nico hated Lorenzo so much."

"I can't lie. I went through a period of time when I hated Lorenzo, too."

"When I met him last night, he seemed like a decent man. Am I wrong, is he an asshole?"

"No. I actually somewhat like Lorenzo now and he really does love you. I initially hated him because for a very long time, I blamed him for you and Supreme getting a divorce. It wasn't his fault. It took me awhile to accept that, but once I did, I supported the relationship. Nico never did. You have to understand something, mom. In Nico's mind, if you weren't with Supreme he always thought you would be with him. When you ended up with

Lorenzo, it was like a slap in the face to him. Nico never thought he would have another rival for you heart."

"That makes a lot of sense. Dear daughter, thank you for the insight."

"Anytime, my dear."

"I did call you over because I wanted to talk to you about something else."

"Sounds serious."

"Very serious. The other day, I was having lunch with Skylar in the city. When we got back in the car a man wearing a ski mask was in the backseat with a gun."

"What!" I leaped forward in my chair. My heart began thumping hard at the idea of my mom having another brush with death.

"Yes, but luckily I was driving your father's car and got ahold of his gun. I killed the gunman."

"Good. I'm sick of these motherfuckers fuckin' wit' our family. They all need to die."

"Trust me, that's what your father and Genesis are working on right now. Trying to figure out how to get rid of whoever is behind this."

"What about the gunman, did you get any

information on him?"

"No. He had no id and I blew off half his face, so he was unrecognizable. I want to put some guards on you, to be on the safe side."

"It's already been done."

"So soon? Nico works fast."

"Not dad, Amir."

"Amir?" my mother asked, with her face full of confusion.

"I didn't want to say anything, because you had only been home from the hospital for a short period of time. You didn't need any additional stress."

"Tell me what happened?"

"A man wearing a ski mask ran up in the apartment and tried to knock me out with chloroform. I think he was trying to kidnap me. I managed to get away and he ran out before I shot him. I didn't kill him but he was hit."

After telling my mother the story, I wondered if her gunman and my gunman was one in the same. It was too bad she wasn't able to see his face, because I could've at least found out if his description matched the man Maya was talking to at the party. But no such luck.

"Aaliyah, you should've told us."

"I did tell Amir, and he put a few of his men on me. I'm fine, you're fine—thank goodness—but we need to figure this out soon. I don't want anything to happen to you again," I said, reaching my hand over to hold my mother's.

"We'll get through it as a family, because I don't want anything to happen to you, either," my mother said, as we held hands.

Precious

Nico stood on the balcony in our bedroom that overlooked the swimming pool. He had been so distant since Amir's birthday party and I had to find a way to reach him.

"Has Genesis had any luck finding out who that man was that I shot?"

"None. All we can do is beef up security until we figure all this shit out."

"When are we going to make time to figure our shit out?"

"There is nothing to figure out...everything is good between us."

"Nico, you haven't touched me since the party. We need to talk about it."

"I don't want to."

"Why?"

"Why talk about something when there is no solution."

"What are you talking about? There's always a solution."

"You know why I don't want to touch you, because I'm afraid."

"Afraid of what?"

"That one day you'll wake up and you'll no longer be mine."

"Nico, that's not gonna happen. I'm in love with you. I'm committed to you and our relationship. What do I have to do to prove it to you?"

"There's nothing you can do. I keep reminding myself that before the shooting, you weren't in love with me, you were in love with somebody else."

"That life doesn't exist for me anymore. It's been months and I still don't remember. At this point, I don't even care about remembering. I'm truly happy with you and whomever I loved before, I don't love anymore. It's time for you to have more faith in the love that we share. If you don't, we won't make it, and it won't be because of Supreme or

Lorenzo, it will be because of you."

Nico stepped off the balcony, leaving me standing there alone. I shook my head in frustration, tired of him walking away. There was nothing worse fighting for something and the other person resisting your efforts every step. I was ready to lift up one of the chairs and throw it over the balcony, ready to release my own rage.

"I don't know how much more of this I..." before I could finish my sentence, Nico was now standing in front of me, on bended knee.

"This is the ring you gave me when you asked me to marry you years ago."

"Yes, it is."

"I thought when you said you had it, you were only trying to keep me calm, while I was in the hospital."

"No. I was telling the truth. I always kept it. I was never able to part with it, but I would love to put it back on your finger. Will you marry me?"

"Yes! Yes! Yes! I would marry you today. You truly are the love of my life," I said, staring at the ring. *The sparkler was more beautiful and even bigger than I remembered* I thought, staring down at my hand, anxious for Nico to put it on.

"And you are mine." After Nico slipped the ring on my finger, we kissed for what felt like an eternity.

"We're getting married. It's long overdue," Nico said, laying me down on the bed. I had my man back and soon he would be my husband. Life couldn't get any better than this.

"Congratulations on your engagement. You have made Nico a very happy man," Genesis said, when he greeted me.

"And he has made me a very happy woman."

"So, when is the wedding?"

"He wants to get married as soon as possible and so do I. I've narrowed it down to three wedding planners. I'm hoping to make my decision by the end of the week, so we can have a summer nuptial."

"The summer ends in a couple months."

"I know, that means we have to move fast."

"I really am happy for you, Precious. Nico, too, but especially you."

"Why especially me?"

"Because, what would amount to setbacks to

most people, you keep moving forward, becoming a better woman each time."

"Thank you for saying that, but I'm not the only one that deserves to be happy, so do you. How are things between you and Skylar?"

"The incident that happened a couple weeks ago really shook her up."

"Has she changed her mind about moving to New York?"

"No, she wants to move forward with our relationship, but now I'm having second thoughts."

"You don't think she can cope?"

"Nope," Genesis conceded, leaning back on his desk. "She keeps saying she can handle it, but her mouth is saying one thing and her eyes are speaking something entirely different. Then, her son, he's only two. I don't know if I'm ready to be responsible for their lives. I mean, I could protect them to the fullest and one of my enemies could still manage to get to them. There's no guarantees with this shit."

"Genesis, there is no guarantee in life, period. The same way this street life could be Skylar's downfall, so could a horrible car accident, or a fatal disease. The point is, as long as you're living your life, there's a chance it can be taken away. That's why you have to live each day to the fullest and if you're able to find someone that makes each day you're living better, then it's worth trying to make it work."

"Aren't you the same woman that was scolding me about my relationship with Skylar? Now, you're endorsing it, why the change?"

"I do have my concerns about Skylar, but I believe she cares deeply for you and it's obvious she makes you happy. Your life is dangerous, but she's well aware of that. I asked Skylar point blank if she was ready for the ugliness that might come from her being in your life and she said you were worth the risk. Even after we were held up and I had to shoot that man, yes, Skylar was scared, but she wasn't deterred. You're aware of the saying 'you only live once', that applies to you, too."

"I do want to see where things can go between me and Skylar, but I'ma wait before I move her here."

"Wait for what?"

"Wait until we figure out who the fuck is determined to take down our organization. Knowing that somebody wants to destroy us, but we can't put a face to it is really fuckin' wit' me."

"Still no leads?"

"Nope, and even though I didn't want him to know what was going on, I even reached out to our Mexican connect, to see if he heard anything from one of his other buyers."

"What did he say?"

"He was adamant that he hadn't heard a thing, but would keep his ears open and keep me posted, if anything changes."

"Whoever it is, is hell-bent on seeing this through. They are not letting up."

"That's why I can't bring Skylar here, yet. She needs to stay in L.A. with her son, until it's at least somewhat safe. Mentally, all my focus has to be on business. I don't need any distractions."

I respected what Genesis was saying and in a lot of ways, I agreed with it, but I seriously doubted Skylar would be so understanding. She was looking forward to starting her life over in New York with Genesis, and even having a gun pointed to her head hadn't changed her mind. I had a feeling Skylar wouldn't take Genesis change of heart, without putting up a formidable fight.

Aaliyah

"Married...you're getting married?" I repeated, as I stood in the middle of the shoe section in Henri Bendel, with my mouth wide open, after seeing the diamond engagement ring on my mother's finger. When she suggested we have a mother/daughter day filled with shopping, the spa, and a mani/pedi, never did I think she would drop the marriage bomb.

"I thought you would be happy for us."

"I am."

"You don't sound like it."

"I guess I'm shocked. I hope this is going to be a long engagement."

"No, we're getting married in a couple of months."

"Let me sit down. You're throwing a lot at me right now. You only got shot a few months ago. You haven't even given yourself time to regain your memory."

"What if I never regain it? Am I supposed to stop living my life, hoping that one day I'll wake up and everything will be the way that it was? Don't you get it? Nothing will ever be the same and I don't want it to be. I'm happy."

"Mom, I love you so much and I want you to be happy, I really do, but this is so soon. I'm worried."

"Aaliyah, don't worry about me. Getting shot might've put my life on a different path, but my new journey is amazing. You need to embrace it, I have."

I stared into my mother's eyes. They were so full of vivacity. For the first time that I could remember, her inner beauty was equally aligned to her outer beauty. In my heart, as much as I loved Nico, I didn't believe my mother's final destiny ended with him, but this was her journey to take, and I would support it to the very end.

"So, wait, you came up with nothing on Maya?"

"Nada. She's as clean as a whistle. You were wrong. Are you going to be able to get those words out of your mouth?"

"Amir, don't make me toss this drink in your face."

"Don't get mad at me because you let your paranoia get the best of you. Maybe now you'll give your Aunt Maya a chance."

"I haven't had enough drinks to entertain your jokes."

"I wasn't joking. Your mother seems to be getting close to Maya. It might be time for you to accept it."

"I would have to see Maya walk on water before I accepted anything positive about her. Maybe I was wrong..."

"Say that again," Amir mocked.

"Maybe I was wrong about Maya having something to do with the bullshit going on with our family, but that doesn't mean she still isn't diabolical. Enough about Maya though, we've hit yet another dead-end. We're no closer to finding my mother's shooter than when it first happened."

"When you least expect it, we'll find out the truth."

"I need that truth to be revealed ASAP or I'm about to start killing people, just because."

"What happened to you?"

"Excuse me...what type of question is that?"

"You were always spoiled and self-centered, but now you're cold. You weren't like that before, or maybe it's your new boyfriend, Dale's fault. He's turned you into some drug queen pin, with no heart."

"How 'bout we make a deal. I won't talk about that crazy, tragic girlfriend of yours, Latreese, and you keep Dale's name out of your mouth."

"Oh, you can dish shit, but you can't take it."

"Can't take what?"

"The truth about how fucked up you've become."

"I'm fucked up? Go, take a look in the mirror. You runnin' 'round here wit' a wannabe bougie broad that's so far up yo' ass, she can't even find her own identity. But I forget, that's how you like your women. You want them to play games and pretend they're good girls and will speak only when spoken to. Unlike me, who keeps shit extra real. You can't handle my mouth, motherfucker."

"Aaliyah, fuck you."

"That's all you got for a rebuttal. Not surprised, you're so transparent," I said, gulping down the last of my drink. "I've lost my appetite. When my food comes, you can take it to go, 'cause I'm done here."

I left the restaurant steaming. The nerve of Amir, bashing my man and me when he was carrying around that tacky luggage named Latreese. One thing he would get no argument from me about was that I had changed. I was framed for a murder I didn't commit, spent months in jail, and felt that my loved ones had turned their backs on me, when I was locked up. If that doesn't bring about change, I don't know what the fuck would.

So, no, I wasn't the teenage girl with my head in the clouds that Amir adored. I was a grown woman that had experienced some real life bullshit, who no longer believed in fairytales, Santa Clause, and the motherfuckin' tooth fairy. If Amir wanted to hold on to virginal Aaliyah, then so be it, he could eat dust.

Precious

Two Months Later...

“I can’t believe this day is finally here. I’m getting married to the love of my life,” I said, staring at myself in the full-length mirror. I felt like a real life princess in my Monique Lhuillier dress. The floating corded leaf with embroidered circular lace gave the romantic strapless mermaid gown an ethereal touch, but my favorite part was the organza and lace details, accented by crystal and embroidery at the hip.

“You really do look gorgeous, mom.”

“Thank you. Now, I need the final touch,” I said, picking up the diamond tiara that was a wedding gift from Nico. Now, I really did look like a princess. In the reflection from the mirror, I caught Aaliyah wiping her eyes.

"Why are you crying?" I asked turning around to face her.

"I'm not crying. I was just getting something out of my eye."

"Aaliyah, tell me the truth," I said taking her hand.

"These last several months have been crazy. It's like I lost my mother, now I have you back, but it's a new you. I guess I'm crying because I still haven't gotten over losing the old you. I miss her, so much."

"I know, baby, and I'm sorry."

"No, you're not."

"Why would you say that?"

"Like you said, you're marrying the love of your life. Which is also crazy to me, because growing up, you always said daddy was the love of your life."

I put my head down thinking about what Aaliyah said. After all this time, I had no recollection of the great love I shared with Supreme. It was almost bizarre to me that I felt like I was getting married for the very first time, even after looking at the ton of pictures from me and Supreme's wedding. Now, I was about to walk down the aisle with Nico, the only man I remember being in love with.

"I understand this is hard on you, your brother, and even Supreme, but I'm here, I'm alive, and I feel so blessed to have a second chance to be with my family, and marry the man that I love. I know it's not the man that everybody thinks I'm supposed to be with, but he's the only man my heart knows."

"I get that."

"I know you miss the old me, but we're building new memories together. I may not remember our previous life, but I do know I love you and your brother more than anything. I'm so proud to be your mother. I love you, Aaliyah."

"I love you too," she said, as we shared a long embrace. "Now, we have to stop crying. We're ruining our makeup." We both laughed, before hugging again.

"Are you two ready?" Quentin said, coming into the room.

"Yes, grandfather, I believe my mother is ready." Aaliyah gave me a certain smile, as if letting me know she was finally okay with this wedding taking place.

"Yes, I am."

"Good, because so am I. I feel honored to walk my daughter down the aisle. This is truly one of the happiest days of my life."

"Let's get out of here, before you get all choked up," I laughed, grabbing my bouquet.

"Daddy, what are you doing here?" I heard Aaliyah say.

"Nico, get out! You know it's bad luck to see the bride before she's about to walk down the aisle," I screamed out, keeping my back turned.

"Mom, it's not Nico."

I turned around and saw Supreme standing in the doorway. For some strange reason, I felt butterflies in my stomach. In my mind, I reasoned it had to be the excitement of getting married.

"I apologize for interrupting, but I was hoping I could get a few moments alone with the bride," Supreme said. Aaliyah and Quentin looked at each other and then at me, waiting for my response.

"Sure, that's fine."

"We'll be right outside, Precious," Quentin said, heading out with Aaliyah. She stopped and gave Supreme a kiss on the cheek, before leaving.

"You look absolutely beautiful. Almost as beautiful as the day we got married," Supreme smiled. "I'm kidding, you look just as beautiful."

"Would you stop, you're making me blush."

"That's not my intention. I came because although you don't need it, I wanted to give you my blessing."

"Really?"

"Yes. All I've ever wanted was for you to be happy. If marrying Nico makes you happy, then I wish you nothing but the best."

"Supreme, I don't know what to say. From everything I heard, at one time, we shared this incredible life together. You were my one great love and I can only imagine how it must make you feel that I don't remember any of it. For you to come and give me your blessing lets me know what an amazing man you must be. Whoever you do end up with, she's going to be one lucky lady."

"But she won't be you. There will always be only one Precious Cummings." I felt my eyes watering up, after Supreme said that, and all I could think was *not this again*. The last thing I wanted to do was cry. This was supposed to be one of the happiest days of my life, but a cloud of sadness kept hovering over me. I didn't know what to say. As if reading my mind, Supreme walked over to me and put his finger over my lips. "You don't have to say a word." Supreme kissed me softly on my cheek, before saying, "Goodbye, Precious."

As I watched Supreme walking away, for the first time I felt some sort of real emotional connection to him. It was so weird. It didn't feel like love, but it was something. I decided to brush it off. I had a wedding to attend. I was a bride and my groom was waiting.

Aaliyah

I stood in the garden at the palatial estate that the wedding was being held. What originally was supposed to be small and intimate had turned into a lavish affair. My mother might have lost her memory, but pink was still her favorite color and it showed with the décor. The soft pink color palette was even the tint of my Vera Wang gown. There were over 10,000 flowers, a mix of white roses, pink peonies, and hydrangeas. It was opulent and girlie, exactly the way my mother wanted it.

In the midst of my thoughts, I heard the music begin to play and knew that was my cue to begin my stroll down the aisle. I smiled at the many faces staring back at me. The loosely hanging pink flowers accenting the chairs seemed to guide me towards my final destination. Once I reached it, there was Nico. Throughout all the years, this was truly the happiest I had ever seen my dad.

When the music began playing for the bride's arrival, every eye was on my mother. It was as if time stopped. She looked stunning holding her bouquet of flowers, with a sparkly diamond wrap, as the long train on her dress floated behind her. She glided down the aisle that was highlighted with a striking petal design. The petals led to the altar, which was adorned with pink and white roses, cascading crystals, and an antique chandelier. She stepped through the ivory drapery, on the pillars that overlooked the lake, to exchange vows with my dad.

Once my grandfather gave my mother's hand to Nico, a single tear fell down his face. My mother wiped it away and whispered something to him. I had never seen my father cry before. It was like he had dreamed of this moment for so long and felt blessed that he would finally be able to call my mother his wife. There wasn't a single dry eye as the two of them recited their own vows of love and devotion. Once they were pronounced man and wife, the guests erupted with cheers. As much as I wanted my mom and Supreme to get back together and live happily ever after, even I had to admit that this felt meant to be.

"I'm so happy for both of you. It was such a beautiful wedding and reception."

"I have to agree with Aaliyah. I've been to a few weddings and this has to be the best one yet," Genesis said, walking up to us. "I wouldn't expect anything other than the best from the two of you. I know I've said it a few times already, but congratulations. True love prevailed."

"Yes, it did," Nico said, kissing my mother. "We've been given a second chance at having a life together and this time we're going to get it right. Nothing will come between us. This will be our happily ever after."

"Cheers to that," my mom beamed, lifting up her champagne glass. As my mom, dad, and Genesis laughed and talked it up, I didn't notice Amir coming towards us, until he grabbed my arm, pulling me off to the side.

"Is this really necessary?" I snapped, yanking my arm out of his grasp.

"I need to talk to you."

"Obviously, but you don't need to strong arm me to get your words out. Just speak."

"Yeah, I can speak, but it don't mean shit if you're not listening, which it seems you never are."

"Amir, we're at my parent's wedding. This is supposed to be a celebration. I'm not about to be arguing with you today. If you want to fight, call me tomorrow. I might be up for it then."

"Listen, I don't want to fight with you."

"Then what do you want?"

"Remember, you had thought Maya was up to something? So, I had my men watch her moves and record her phone conversations."

"Yeah, you came up with nothing and dismissed me as being paranoid."

"Your paranoia might have some validity to it."

"Why do you say that?"

"I just got a call. Maya has been very clever about it, but she's been in touch with a man by the name of Arnez."

"Who is Arnez? Should I be familiar with that name?"

"A couple days ago, one of my workers told me the name, I didn't recognize it either, but I had him do a little digging, because it seemed Maya was heavily intertwined with this mystery man."

"What did he find out?"

"Arnez is not only extremely dangerous, but he's also supposed to be dead."

"Dead. What dealings would Maya have going on with him?"

"Whatever it is, it can't be good."

My face frowned; thinking about what Maya could be scheming on. I wanted to be wrong, but it seemed she was up to the same bullshit, per usual. Whatever it was, we needed to get to the bottom of it fast.

"Your worker couldn't get any other specifics?"

"Not yet, but he's still on it. I have a really bad feeling about this, though. We've crossed the brothers off the list of suspects for ordering the hit at the warehouse. So, it has to be someone that had just enough access to get the necessary information about the location and who would be there."

"How would Maya get that, though? None of us fuck with her. At least, my mom wasn't back then." Right after I said that, Amir and I both turned in the same direction. "Grandfather. And Maya is over there right now, all in his face with her fake smile, playing up to him."

"Yep. Maya got the info from Quentin, without him even realizing she was playing him."

"I'm going over there right now to put Maya's trifling ass on blast, before I drag her out of this reception."

"Not yet." Amir said, pulling my arm. "Let's see if the worker can find out some more dirt, first. If we bring it to the table now, Maya will talk her way out the bullshit once again."

"True, because grandfather always wants to give that psycho daughter of his the benefit of the doubt. With my mother losing her memory, even she has put her guard down, with that snake sister of hers."

"That's why we have to come fully equipped, with all our ammunition. If we can prove that Maya was working with Arnez, and they're responsible for what happened at the warehouse, not even Quentin will be able to save his daughter's life this time."

"Let's continue discussing these new developments after we leave, because my mom and dad are coming this way."

"Hey, we're about to head out," my mother said, giving me a hug.

"Already?"

"What do you mean already? We've been partying for hours. We need to catch our flight."

"You're taking a private jet. That flight isn't

going anywhere."

"No doubt, but your mother and I are ready to start our honeymoon," my dad said, wrapping his arms around my mother's tiny waist. They were acting like two high school lovebirds. It was actually really cute. For a brief moment, I thought about how I used to feel that way about Amir, but quickly brushed it off.

"Well, I'm not going to try and stop you lovebirds from your honeymoon. I'm going to miss you both while you're gone, but I want you to have an amazing time."

"We plan on it," my mom blushed. As Genesis and my grandfather saw them about to leave, everybody started walking towards the entrance, to send them off. I had to muster up all my strength not to slap the shit out of Maya, when she came trailing along behind the crowd with her bullshit hugs and kisses. Guests were getting their cars from the valet and we all made small talk, while waiting for the driver to bring my parent's ride to the front.

When we noticed the car pulling up, my dad lifted my mother off the ground and started swinging her around. She was giggling non-stop like a little girl.

"Don't drop her," Genesis joked. Everybody

laughed. I felt like in some way, all of us were relishing in their happiness it seemed contagious. So contagious, that instead of paying attention to our surroundings, all eyes were focused on the newlyweds. To the point that no one noticed the tinted minivan driving by, until the M16's started blasting out the windows.

"Everybody get down!" Genesis barked, as everyone ran for cover. The bullets rang out for a few seconds and then we heard tires screeching off. "Nobody move!" Genesis yelled out again, I figured he wanted to make sure the shooters were gone before standing up and getting caught in the line of fire. After a couple minutes of only hearing people breath hard, we all began rising up believing we were in the clear.

"Is everybody okay?" grandfather asked, looking around. I immediately ran over to my mother, who was lying on the ground next to my father.

"Are you guys alright!" I screamed, turning my mother's body over, thinking I was going to see her lying in a pool of blood.

"We're fine," my dad stuttered, helping my mother up. "When I heard the bullets, I rushed to get your mother down to the ground, so I could cover her and we tripped over the step. We fell on this damn concrete," Nico explained, rubbing his forehead.

"Precious, are you okay? Do you need to go to the hospital?"

"No, I'm good. Just have a little headache, but I'm fine. Really, I am," my mother insisted, as everybody was surrounding her, making sure she wasn't hurt.

"What the hell is going on?" Genesis said, shaking his head. "Nobody was supposed to get past the gates to this estate, without an invite."

"Do you think they shot the guard up front?" I asked.

"I don't know. I sent some of my men up there to check."

"The bigger question is how you pull up with machine guns, yet nobody gets hit. Not one person," Amir said. "I don't care how fast we ducked down, somebody should've caught a bullet."

"Unless that wasn't the shooters intention," grandfather reasoned.

"If them showing up with guns blazing wasn't to kill anybody, then what was the point?" I wanted to know.

"Maybe it was a warning. Letting us know that they could get to us anytime they wanted," Genesis said, putting his hands over his head, as he paced back and forth.

"So, somebody is fuckin' wit' us. Trying to play head games."

"Nico, that's exactly what I'm thinking," my grandfather confirmed.

I looked over at Amir and he was staring me dead in my face. I knew we were both thinking the same thing. From the corner of our eyes we both zeroed in on Maya who was holding my grandfather's hand. It was time for Maya to die.

Precious

"You really didn't have to spend the night, Aaliyah."

"I know, but I was worried about you."

"I went to the emergency room last night and they gave me every test known to man. I'm fine."

"You've been through so much these last few months. You can't push too hard."

"I thought I was supposed to be the mother. You worry way too much, but I love you for it."

"I just want you to relax."

"I want the same. That's why my bags are packed and I'm ready to board this jet. I wish Nico would hurry up, so we can go," I said, eyeing my watch.

"Did he say when he would be back?"

"Shortly was all he said, before leaving. Genesis called him this morning, so I think his disappearance is business related. Like you, your father doesn't want me stressing, so of course, he didn't discuss any of it with me."

"I understand he's concerned about your well-being, like all of us."

"I will be so happy when everybody stops babying me. I haven't felt this good since....well, you know what I mean. The point is, I'm a lot stronger than you all give me credit for. I lost my memory, not my strength."

"I believe you. You've already shown us that," Aaliyah laughed.

"I'm glad somebody does." I'm sure Aaliyah could hear the annoyance in my voice. I knew that she, Nico, and everyone else meant well, but all this handholding was going to drive me bat-shit crazy.

"I'm about to tell you this because I know you're still that woman that can handle anything, with brain trauma and all." Aaliyah's comment made me smile. She had such a way with words.

"I really must be an amazing woman to have been blessed with a child like you. Now, tell your mother what you know."

"I'm pretty sure I know why dad went to meet with Genesis?"

"Why?" I asked, very intrigued. "Do tell."

"Yesterday, Amir found out that Maya is deeply involved with a man named Arnez."

"Who is Arnez?'

"A very dangerous man, that's supposed to be dead. Amir has his men doing some deeper investigating. I'm positive he told his father and now Genesis is telling dad."

"Okay, so Maya is dating a shady man. Why does this require an emergency meeting between Genesis and Nico?"

"I know you lost a big chunk of your memory and you don't remember what type of person Maya was, but..."

"You told me she's done some really bad things and Maya admitted to it," I said cutting Aaliyah off. "She's also said that she's changed and Quentin vouched for her."

"That's because grandfather wants to see the good in his psycho daughter, but there is none."

"Aaliyah, I'm about to go on my honeymoon

and I don't want to leave rehashing the past. I think you should let Maya be. Her dating preference has nothing to do with us."

"This isn't the past. We believe Maya is responsible for something that is happening right now."

"Explain."

"We believe Maya helped orchestrate the hit at the warehouse that almost got you killed and also, the gunshot spectacle at your wedding reception."

"Are you sure?"

"We're still gathering the evidence, but my gut is telling me yes."

"So, you have no evidence. Why would Maya be a part of that?"

"Maya is a sick, devious monster. She's been using your memory loss to become close to you, but yet she's still out to destroy you."

"I don't know, Aaliyah. Maya seems genuine with wanting to have a good relationship with me. This doesn't feel right."

"Of course it doesn't feel right. Anything that has to do with that nut is always cringe worthy, but her nine lives are finally up. We're going to handle

Maya, once and for all."

"Aaliyah, don't."

"Don't what?"

"Don't do anything to Maya just yet."

"Why? She's gotten away with everything, including murder. Enough, already! It's time for Maya to pay up."

"Just wait until your dad and I get back from our honeymoon. Please."

"For what? I want to have good news to share, once you return. Being able to say Maya is dead would be it."

"I have to be able to speak to your grandfather before Maya is killed. He needs to hear it from me. Nico just sent me a text saying he'll be here in a few. We're about to catch this flight, so I'll talk to Quentin, as soon as I get back."

"I don't know, mom."

"Aaliyah, we'll only be gone for ten days. You can wait that long. I'm sure you all have men following Maya, so she won't be able to make any moves, without you being two steps ahead."

"I'm not feeling this whole waiting idea you have."

"Do it for your grandfather. Let's say everything is true about Maya, he's still going to have to bury his daughter. This has to be handled carefully."

"Fine, but Maya will die and even grandfather can't save her this time."

"Just promise me you won't touch Maya, until I get back...promise me, Aaliyah."

"I promise."

"Thank you," I said, giving my daughter a hug.

I detested leaving for my honeymoon with this darkness lingering in the air. I knew one of the main reasons I wanted Aaliyah to wait was because I was hoping she was wrong and within these ten days, they would figure that out.

My memory loss had pushed me away from people that I once loved, but it also brought me closer to others, like Quentin and Maya. I couldn't help but think about the smile on Quentin's face, when he had both of his daughter's together at dinner only a few weeks ago. For his sake, I prayed Aaliyah was wrong about Maya, because I didn't think Quentin could survive the heartache of burying his child.

"I can't believe we're finally here," I gasped, taking in the pristine waters and majestic beaches that surrounded us on the private island.

"Yeah, it took a minute, but it was worth it," Nico said, putting our luggage down. We didn't bring much, because we planned on spending the majority of our time either lounging on the beach, or in bed. I stepped out on our over-the-water bungalow and took in the breathtaking lagoons, an au-natural setting on Bora Bora Island, in French Polynesia. There were no words to describe just how beautiful the island was. It was as if you were getting a little piece of heaven, right here on earth.

"So, what do you want to do on our first day here? Maybe scuba diving and snorkeling."

"I was thinking we could make love, then have the chef come and make us a delicious meal, drink a bottle of their best champagne, and then make love again," Nico suggested, as he walked up from behind and wrapped his arms around me, before sprinkling my neck with kisses.

"Say no more, your wish is my command."

"Is that right, Mrs. Carter?"

"Yes, it is, and please, call me that again."

"Mrs. Carter, my wife. I still can't believe this finally happened for us. I've wanted you to be my wife since that day I saw you struttin' down the street in Harlem, like you owned that motherfucker. I knew then you had to be my queen."

"That was so many years ago, yet it seems like only yesterday. I remember everything about that moment. I tried to give you a hard time, but..."

"Tried?" Nico said, cutting me off. "You did give me a hard time. You had me out there feeling like I was some bum nigga."

"No, I didn't."

"Yes, the fuck you did." We both laughed.

"Okay, I was playing hard to get, but in my head, all I kept saying was how fine you was."

"Is that right?"

"Yep, and you know what Mr. Carter. You're just as fine now as you were then," I said, moving towards Nico slowly, before our lips touched and we began kissing. Nico lifted me up, to carry me over to the plush bed that had white everything. I kept thinking that I couldn't believe I loved him now more than ever. Not only did my heart still skip a beat for him, but also he gave me those butterflies that only your soulmate could.

That day, we made love over and over again, like it was our first time. We skipped out on the chef cooked meal and champagne. Instead, during the brief moments we were able to pull ourselves away from each other's grasp, we ate the fresh fruit and delicatessens that had already been stocked for us, upon our arrival.

With the double doors that led to the beach wide open, the warm sweet breeze and the sounds of the waves crashing had us completely seduced. We couldn't have left our bungalow, even if we wanted to. Our love and passion was holding us hostage and I savored every second of it.

"Precious, I have never been in love with another woman, other than you and I never will," Nico whispered in my ear, as our bodies and minds became one. We continued making love, until we fell asleep in each other's arms.

The remnants of a dream were being chased

away by the tapping sunlight against my face, waking me. I yawned, but my eyes remained closed, as I fought to get back to the peacefulness of my sleep. I'd blink and then shut my eyes, before blinking again. I was losing the battle of going back to that peaceful place.

"Good morning, beautiful," I heard a voice say.

"Where am I," I mumbled, not completely focusing, as I struggled to completely wake up from my deep sleep.

"I know I put it on you all day and night but it was so good, I made you forget where you at? Damn, after all these years, I still got skills."

"Nico," I muttered, as the bright sunlight now had my eyes widening open.

"Yes, sleepyhead. Wake up, so we can have breakfast on the beach."

"Nico!" I screamed, jumping up from the bed. I grabbed the sheet, pulling it off the mattress, and then wrapped it around my naked body. "What the hell are you doing here and where is my husband?" I belted.

"You're so cute. I love how you still like to play practical jokes," Nico laughed.

"Do you see me laughing? Why in the hell are we in the bed naked together? I'm a married woman," I yelled, flashing the enormous rock on my finger. "If Supreme finds out we spent the night together, he will kill me and you. Fuck, I have to call my husband. Where's my phone?" I said looking around.

As I was scrambling around the room, I could feel Nico's eyes burning through me. I tried to ignore him, as all I wanted to do was find my phone, so I could call Supreme, but Nico's intense glare had me uneasy.

"Would you please stop staring at me and help me find my fuckin' phone! I don't know what went down between us last night, but let's pretend it didn't happen. Supreme can never find out about this. Do you understand, Nico? Don't just sit there, say something," I roared, ready to knock the smug look off of his face.

"Precious, I am your husband. We got married day before yesterday. That ring you're wearing is the one I put on your finger. And the one I have on," Nico said, raising his hand, showing a sleek diamond wedding band, "Is the ring you put on mine."

I swallowed hard, before sitting down on the floor trying to process what Nico said. None of this was making any sense to me. There was no way I could be married to Nico, when I was in love with Supreme.

"I don't know what type of sick joke you're playing Nico, but I want no parts of it. I wouldn't marry you; I'm married to Supreme. We share a family together. I love him and he loves me. So, take me home. Take me home to my family and my husband, now!"

Aaliyah

The warm, summer breeze had my body feeling at peace, as I drove through Manhattan, in my drop top white Bentley. Although the beautiful weather had my body feeling one way, it was doing absolutely nothing to calm my mind. I was on my way to meet Dale for lunch, and instead of looking forward to seeing my man, the Maya situation had me zoning out.

I was waiting for Amir to get back to me with more details regarding her relationship with Arnez and who he was, but so far nothing. I even called him a couple times, but he kept sending me to voicemail. I figured, for whatever reason, Amir was trying to now keep me out the loop. That was a no go for me.

After my lunch date with Dale, I planned on making a beeline straight to Amir.

When I pulled up to the restaurant, the valet took my car and I headed straight through the double glass doors to meet with Dale. I didn't even bother waiting for the hostess to seat me, because from a distance, I could see Dale sitting at a corner booth. It wasn't until I got right up to the table did I see his brother, Emory.

"What the fuck is he doing here," I snapped, so loudly that half the restaurant had turned in our direction.

"Aaliyah, keep your voice down," Dale said, putting his hand on top of mine firmly. My eyes stayed glued on Emory. I couldn't stand the motherfucker, point blank, period. I sat down, deciding it was unnecessary to bring anymore unwanted attention to us.

"I'ma keep my voice down, but I still want to know why is your brother here?" I asked, taking a seat across from them.

"I thought we were past all of this," Emory said, taking a sip of his water.

"Past what...me not liking you? Nah, that's an

ongoing thing."

"Aaliyah, I thought we all agreed to put our past issues behind us and move forward. So, why do you still have beef with Emory?"

"I don't trust him," I said, snarling in Emory's direction.

"At this point, this dislike thing has become mutual, but my brother has made it clear the two of you are an item, and I must respect your relationship. Because of the love I have for my brother, I'm trying my best to mend this broken relationship we have, but you're making it very difficult."

"Does it look like I care?"

"Aaliyah, can you just hear him out?" Dale implored. I didn't verbalize a response. I simply sat up straight in my seat, faking like Emory had my full attention.

"As I was saying, I'm trying to mend our relationship. I think finding out who actually hired Tori to infiltrate your family's business would be a good start."

"Yeah, it would, but with Tori being dead, I thought the truth died with her."

"So did we, but I think we might have a major

breakthrough."

"What kind of breakthrough?" I questioned, sitting extra straight up in my chair. This time, I wasn't pretending like Emory had my full attention, he actually did.

"Do you know a man named Arnez Douglass?"

My heart began racing when Emory dropped that name. In my head, I quickly debated whether I should come clean and admit that Amir mentioned him being linked to Maya, and was having that further investigated, or should I play dumb. I opted on playing clueless. Technically, I didn't know anything about this Arnez character and needed to get all the dirt I could get.

"No, who is that?"

"He was a major player in the drug game a few years ago. He moved a ton of weight out in Atlanta, before he got killed. I guess his death was greatly exaggerated, because he's been making serious moves behind the scenes. While Tori was supposed to be working with us to infiltrate the Dominican family, she was also working for Arnez. He is the one that's responsible for that hit put on your family and for causing this beef we had with the Dominicans. Arnez is orchestrating all this shit, hoping we'll wipe each other out and he'll be the last motherfucker standing, and take over each of our territories, including your families."

I sat speechless for a few minutes. Everything Emory said made perfect sense. The only piece missing was Maya's role. They probably weren't aware that Arnez had more than just Tori on his payroll, but for now they didn't need to know.

"Aaliyah, are you okay?" Dale asked, touching my arm, shaking me out of my thoughts.

"Yeah, I'm fine. I'm just trying to take in everything Emory said."

"I know it's a lot, but I checked the info and it's all accurate."

"No…no…I'm not doubting what your brother said, I believe him."

"Really?" Emory sounded stunned. With our history I couldn't blame him. "I figured you would throw a ton of questions my way, in an attempt to discredit me and make me out to be a liar."

"Normally I would, because you give me reason to doubt you, but this time is different. I believe you're sincerely making an attempt to gain my trust."

"I hope you truly believe that, because I am." I wasn't completely sold on this new and somewhat improved Emory, but I decided it was better for me to have both of the brothers on my side. Two was definitely more powerful than one.

"Like I said, I believe you are. Now that we got that out the way, let's discuss the most important thing. How do we get to Arnez? I need him dead like yesterday."

"He's been doing an excellent job at keeping himself underground for the last few years. We have to come up with a plan to bring him out of hiding. Besides Tori, he must have some help, because he's making moves even after her death."

"He sure has. Most recently at my parent's wedding reception."

"You didn't tell me something went down at your parent's wedding," Dale said, full of concern.

"Everybody is fine. I was going to tell you today, over lunch."

"So, what happened?" Emory questioned.

"After the reception, when everybody was waiting for their cars to leave, a minivan drove up and just started shooting, but nobody got shot. It was almost as if the shooter was fuckin' wit' us."

"You mean like sending a message that he could get to you."

"Exactly. After what you just told me, I'll put my money on Arnez being behind the shit."

"Still stirring the pot. Shit done cooled down lately, probably tryna get havoc to breakout again."

"Or maybe, Arnez has already plotted on making it happen. Is anything coming up that would be a perfect opportunity for him to strike again?" Dale inquired.

"Not for my family." As I was saying that, I felt my phone vibrate. It was a text from Amir, saying he needed to see me.

"Something's up, we have to figure it out before it blows up in our faces."

"Listen, I have to go. I'll see you later on tonight, baby."

"You have to leave already...where are you going?"

"I told my mother I would meet with this realtor chick while she was gone. She just texted me. I totally forgot and I'm running late," I said, giving Dale a brief kiss.

"Cool, I'll see you later on, but call me if you need me."

"You do the same and Emory, thanks for the information about Arnez. I truly appreciate it," I said, as I waved bye.

"No problem," Emory smiled, as if pleased with himself.

On my way to meet Amir, I focused on my one and only goal, to kill Maya. She was the weakest link. Maya was the one filtering all the information to Arnez. That's how he was able to know where my parent's wedding was being held, even though it had been kept hush-hush. If I got rid of Maya once and for all, I knew that would at least slow Arnez down, until we could take him out permanently.

Right when I was pulling up in front of Amir's building, I saw that Nico was calling me. "Hey daddy. I can't believe you found time to call me on your honeymoon," I laughed.

"Your mother and I are actually on the jet right now, headed home."

"What? You all were supposed to be gone for ten days. What happened?" There was a long silence before Nico finally spoke.

"There were some complications, so we had to cut our trip short. I'll explain once we get back."

"Is my mom okay?"

"Yes. I just wanted to let you know we're on our way back. I'll call you once we land." I could tell my dad was rushing me off the phone, because I didn't even have a chance to say bye before he hung up. I couldn't help but wonder what happened that made them cut their honeymoon so short. Nico said my mother was fine, but his voice was telling me a different story, which had me concerned.

I decided I needed to press the speed button on this Maya situation. I wanted her dead before my mother returned. I didn't need any holdups. To be sure nothing stopped me from accomplishing my goal, Maya would die today.

"I'm glad you were able to get here so quickly," Amir said, when he opened his apartment door.

"I assumed it was important. Did you find out

some additional information about Arnez?"

"Yep. It's worse than I thought."

"What do you mean?"

"Arnez Douglass is responsible for my mother's death and my grandmother. Two women that I never met in my life, but that I love very much."

"Are you serious? What type of sicko is he and how did you find out?"

"When I mentioned his name to my dad, regarding Maya, he filled me in on his entire history with Arnez. Do you know Renny was the one that had supposedly killed him?"

"You're talking about your Aunt Nichellle's husband, Renny?"

"Yes. Arnez is his cousin. There is so much bad blood. I can't believe Maya has aligned herself with him."

"Can you imagine all the damage those two psychopaths can do? Hell, they've already started. We need to get rid of them ASAP, starting with Maya."

"I agree, but my father wants to deal with it, personally. He promised my mother's father everyone that was responsible for her death had been eliminated. He was wrong and he's determined to make it right. This is way above our heads."

"Says who? Your father...my father? It was because of my hunch and you following through on it that led us to this pertinent information. Now that we got the goods, we're supposed to fall back and let the grown folks handle it? Fuck that, we grown too."

"Aaliyah, trust me. Knowing that this Arnez nigga had something to do with my mother's death, I want to kill him my damn self, but my father's right. That man is dangerous and he needs to be handled properly. I don't want to fuck it up and neither should you."

"I have no intentions of fuckin' anything up."

"Good, because I wasn't supposed to tell you any of this, but I thought you should know. Plus, keeping this information to myself was fuckin' my head up."

"Thanks for sharing. I know finding that out about your mother and grandmother had to be difficult for you."

"Although my father keeps them hidden away, because he doesn't like the reminder, I've seen so many pictures of my mother."

"I remembered a long time ago, you showed

me a few. She was so beautiful. You have her eyes and lips."

"I never met her, but I miss her so much. My father has been the best dad, but I can't help but wonder how my life would've been if I had grown up with my mother around, too."

"That's only natural," I said, sitting down next to Amir, "but I'm starting to learn that you can't dwell on things you have no control over. If you do, it'll drive you crazy. Try to put your energy on the things you can change."

"Am I hearing words of wisdom from you?" Amir grinned.

"Maybe."

"You wear maturity well."

"A week from now, remember you said that when you're ready to curse me out, but don't worry if you forget, I'll remind..." before I finished my sentence, Amir leaned in and his tongue was down my throat.

"Amir, what are doing and what about Latreese?" I gasped, pushing him away, "and let's not forget, I'm also taken."

"I'm sorry, Aaliyah...no I'm not."

"Excuse me."

"I've wanted to do that for months, now."

"Our time has passed. We've both moved on, well, at least I have."

"So, you're happy with Dale."

"You almost seem like you're in pain saying his name, but yes, very happy. He gets me…you never did."

"That's not true. I do get you, better than you think. That's why…"

"I hate to cut you off, but I really have to go," I said looking down at my watch, realizing I had to beat it if I wanted to make sure I pulled off my last minute plan for Maya. "Maybe we can continue this conversation another time."

"Where are you rushing off to?"

"I have some things to take care of, before my mom gets back."

"Your mom. She's on her honeymoon with your dad. They won't be back for awhile."

"Not anymore. My dad called when I was on my way over here. They're on the plane, headed back as we speak."

"Why did they cut their trip short?"

"I have no clue, but the point is they did. I need to get some things done before they return."

"Things like what?"

"Just things and why are you questioning me?"

"Because like I just said, I get you."

"And..."

"And, I get the feeling you're up to some bullshit."

"You're wrong, but I don't have time to debate with you. I have to go," I said, grabbing my purse. "Although romance ain't in the cards for us, I still got love for you. So, if you ever want to talk about your mother or anything else that's bothering you, I'm here," I said, before kissing Amir on the cheek.

"You're such a con artist," I heard Amir say, before I slammed the door behind me.

I couldn't get out of Amir's apartment and into my car fast enough. I was heading straight to Maya's place. I unlocked a secret compartment in my vehicle for the two things I needed: my gun and the key to Maya's crib. A long time ago, without his knowledge of course, I took the key from my grandfather and made a copy. I returned it before he even realized it was missing. I knew one day, I would need this key and that day had finally come.

I parked my car around the corner and called Maya's house, to make sure she wasn't home yet. Last week, my grandfather had invited me to some event him and Maya were attending, but I politely turned him down, for obvious reasons. I didn't know the exact time it was over, but from what I remembered my grandfather telling me, the event was still going on. I hoped I was early, so I could be lying in wait for Maya's ass.

Luckily, Maya lived in a brownstone, so there wasn't a doorman who could identify me entering her building. When I stepped inside, I heard what sounded like a television on coming from the back. I proceeded with caution, with my weapon drawn, ready to bust off, if I had to. As I got closer to the bedroom where the sounds were coming from, I stood with my back up against the wall, before quickly turning towards the door entrance. With my finger on the trigger and gun aimed straight ahead, I was ready to start shooting, but nobody was there. I was tempted to cut the television off, so I could hear better, but opted against it. Instead, I decided to head back towards the foyer and as I got closer, I heard the front door opening.

"Death awaits you, Maya," I whispered, ducking into the hallway restroom. The sounds of high heels clicking on the hardwood floor let me know when Maya was getting closer. The moment I heard her passing by, I stepped out, putting the tip of the gun to the back of her head.

"What the hell!" Maya screamed out, before her body jolted.

"It's time for you to die and I have the pleasure of pulling the trigger," I smiled, as my finger began itching, ready to have Maya's brain splatter decorate the taupe colored walls.

"If it isn't the lovely Aaliyah. If you pull that trigger, you better be prepared to die, too," I heard an unknown male voice say to me, as the cold, metal steel sunk into the back of my head.

"Fuck," I mumbled under my breath.

"What's it gonna be...are you gonna live or are you ready to die?"

The Countdown Begins...One More Book In The Series, Until Bitch The Final Chapter!!

A KING PRODUCTION

DRAKE

A NOVEL

JOY DEJA KING

AND CHRIS BOOKER

Prologue

"Push! Push!" the doctor directed Kim, as he held the top of the baby's head, hoping this would be the final push that would bring a new life into the world.

The hospital's delivery room was packed with both Kim and Drake's family, and although the large crowd irritated Drake, he still managed to video record the birth of his son. After four hours of labor, Kim gave birth to a 6.5-pound baby boy, who they already named Derrick Jamal Henson Jr. Drake couldn't help but to shed a few tears of joy, at the new addition to his family, but the harsh reality of his son's safety quickly replaced his joy with anger.

Drake was nobody's angel and beyond his light brown eyes and charming smile, he was one of the most feared men in the City of Philadelphia, due to his street cred. He put a lot of work in on the blocks of South Philly, where he grew up. He mainly pushed drugs and gambled, but from time to time he'd place well-known dealers into the trunk of his car and hold them for ransom, according to how much that person was worth.

"I need everybody to leave the room for awhile." Drake told the people in the hospital room, wanting to share a private moment alone with Kim and his son.

The families took a few minutes saying their goodbyes, before leaving. Kim and Drake sat alone in the room, rejoicing over the birth of baby Derrick. The only interruption was doctors coming in and out of the room, to check up on the baby, mainly because they were a little concerned about his breathing. The doctor informed Drake that he would run a few more tests, to make sure the baby would be fine.

"So, what are you going to do?" Kim questioned Drake, while he was cradling the baby.

"Do about what?" he shot back, without lifting his head up. Drake knew what Kim was alluding to, but he had no interest in discussing it. Once Kim became pregnant, Drake agreed to leave the street life alone, if not completely then significantly cutting back, after their baby was born. They both feared if he didn't stop living that street life, he would land in the box. Drake felt he and jail were like night and day: they could never be together.

"You know what I'm talking about, Drake. Don't play stupid with me," Kim said, poking him in his head with her forefinger.

He smiled. "I gave you my word I was out of the game when you had our baby. Unless my eyes are deceiving me, I think what I'm holding in my arms is our son. Just give me a couple days to clean up the streets and then we can sit down and come up with a plan on how to invest the money we got."

Cleaning up the streets meant selling all the drugs he had and collecting the paper owed to him from his workers and guys he fronted weight to. All together there was about 100-k due, not to mention the fact he had to appoint someone to take over his bread winning crack houses and street corners that made him millions of dollars.

Drake's thoughts came to a halt when his phone started to ring. Sending the call straight to voicemail didn't help any, because it rang again. Right when he reached to turn the phone off, he noticed it was Peaches calling. If it were anybody else, he probably would've declined, but Peaches wasn't just anybody.

"Yo," he answered, shifting the baby to his other arm, while trying to avoid Kim's eyes cutting over at him.

"He knows! He knows everything!" Peaches yelled, with terror in her voice.

Peaches wasn't getting good reception out in the woods, where Villain had left her for dead, so the words Drake was hearing were broken up. All he understood was, "Villain knows!" That was enough to get his heart racing. His heart wasn't racing out of fear, but rather excitement.

In many ways, Villain and Drake were cut from the same cloth. They even both shared tattoos of several teardrops under their eyes. It seemed like gunplay was the only thing that turned Drake on—besides fucking—and when he could feel it in the air, murder was the only thing on his mind.

Drake hung up the phone and tried to call Peaches back, to see if he could get better reception, but her phone went straight to voicemail. Damn! He thought to himself as he tried to call her back repeatedly and block out Kim's voice as she steadily asked him if everything was alright.

"Drake, what's wrong?"

"Nothing. I gotta go. I'll be back in a couple of hours," he said, handing Kim their son.

"How sweet! There's nothing like family!" said a voice coming from the direction of the door.

Not yet lifting his head up from his son to see who had entered the room, at first Drake thought it was a doctor, but once the sound of the familiar voice kicked in, Drake's heart began beating at an even more rapid pace. He turned to see Villain standing in the doorway, chewing on a straw and clutching what appeared to be a gun at his waist. Drake's first instinct was to reach for his own weapon, but remembering that he left it in the car made his insides burn. Surely, if he had his gun on him, there would have been a showdown right there in the hospital.

"Can I come in?" Villain asked, in an arrogant tone, as he made his way over to the visitors' chairs. "Let me start off by saying congratulations on having a bastard child."

Villain's remarks made Drake's jaw flutter continuously from fury. Sensing shit was about to go left, Kim attempted to get out of the bed with her baby to leave the room, but before her feet could hit the floor, Villain pulled out a .50 Caliber Desert Eagle and placed it on his lap. The gun was so enormous that Drake could damn near read off the serial number on the slide. Kim looked at the nurse's button and was tempted to press it.

"Push the button and I'll kill all three of y'all. Scream, and I'ma kill all three of y'all. Bitch," Villian paused, making sure the words sunk in. "if you even blink the wrong way, I'ma kill all three of y'all."

"What the fuck you want?" Drake asked, still trying to be firm in his speech.

"You know, at first, I thought about getting my money back and then killin' you, for setting my brother up wit' those bitches you got working for you. But on my way here I just said, 'Fuck the money!' I just wanna kill the nigga."

Deep down inside, Drake wanted to ask for his life to be spared, but his pride wouldn't allow it. Not even the fact that his newborn son was in the room could make Drake beg to stay alive, which made Villain more eager to lullaby his ass into a permanent sleep.

Villain wanted to see the fear in his eyes before he pulled the trigger, but Drake was a G, and was bound to play that role 'til he kissed death.

A KING PRODUCTION

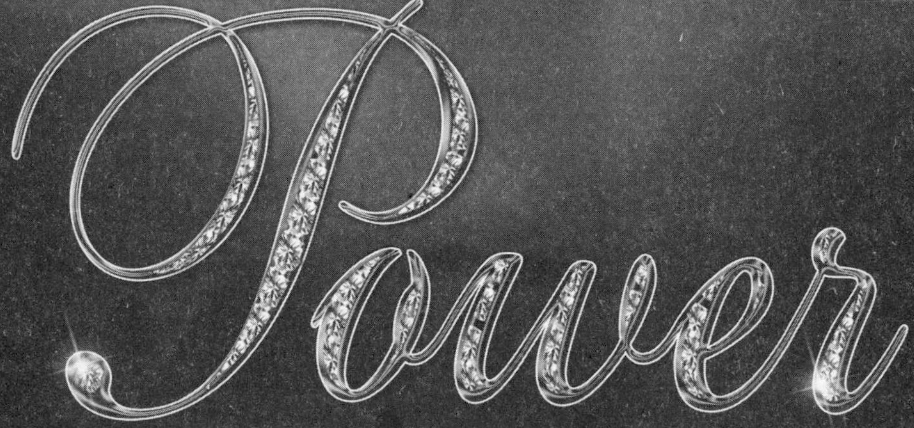

NO ONE MAN SHOULD HAVE ALL THAT POWER...BUT THERE WERE TWO

JOY DEJA KING

Chapter 1

Underground King

Alex stepped into his attorney's office to discuss what his number one priority always was: business. When he sat down, their eyes locked and there was complete silence for the first few seconds. This was Alex's way of setting the tone of the meeting. His silence spoke volumes. This might've been his attorney's office, but he was the head nigga in charge, and nothing got started until he decided it was time to speak. Alex felt this approach was necessary. You see, after all these years of them doing business, attorney George Lofton still wasn't used to dealing with a man like Alex: a dirt-poor kid who could've easily died in the projects he was born in, but instead had made millions. It wasn't done the ski mask way, but it was still illegal.

They'd first met when Alex was a sixteen-year-old kid growing up in TechWood Homes, a housing project in Atlanta. Alex and his best friend, Deion, had been arrested, because the principal found 32 crack vials in Alex's book bag. Another kid had tipped the principal off and the principal subsequently called the police. Alex and Deion were arrested and suspended from school. His mother called George, who had the charges against them dismissed, and they were allowed to go back to school. That wasn't the last time he would use George. He was arrested at twenty-two for attempted murder and for trafficking cocaine a year later. Alex was acquitted on both charges. George Lofton later became known as the best trial attorney in Atlanta, but Alex had also become the best at what he did, and since it was Alex's money that kept Mr. Lofton in designer suits, million dollar homes, and foreign cars, he believed he called the shots, and dared his attorney to tell him otherwise.

Alex noticed that what seemed like a long period of silence made Mr. Lofton feel uncomfortable, which he liked. Out of habit, in order to camouflage the discomfort, his attorney always kept bottled water within arm's reach. He would cough, take a swig, and lean back in his chair, raising his eyebrows a little, trying to give a look of certainty, though he wasn't completely confident at all in Alex's presence. The reason was because Alex did what many had thought would be impossible, especially men like George Lofton. He had gone from a knucklehead, low-level drug dealer to an underground king and an unstoppable, respected criminal boss.

Before finally speaking, Alex gave an intense stare into George Lofton's piercing eyes. They were not only the bluest he had ever seen, but also some of the most calculating. The latter is what Alex found so compelling.

A calculating attorney working on his behalf could almost guarantee a get out of jail free card for the duration of his criminal career.

"Have you thought over what we briefly discussed the other day?" Alex asked his attorney, finally breaking the silence.

"Yes, I have, but I want to make sure I understand you correctly. You want to give me six hundred thousand to represent you or your friend, Deion, if you are ever arrested and have to stand trial again in the future?"

Alex assumed he had already made himself clear, based on their previous conversations, and was annoyed by what he now considered a repetitive question. "George, you know I don't like repeating myself. That's exactly what I'm saying. Are we clear?"

"So, this is an unofficial retainer."

"Yes, you can call it that."

George stood and closed the blinds, then walked over to the door that led to the reception area. He turned the deadbolt, so they wouldn't be disturbed. George sat back behind the desk. "You know that if you and your friend Deion are ever on the same case, that I can't represent the both of you."

"I know that."

"So, what do you propose I do if that was ever to happen?"

"You would get him the next best attorney in Atlanta," Alex said, without hesitation. Deion was Alex's best friend—had been since the first grade. They were now business partners, but the core of their bond was built on that friendship, and because of that, Alex would always look out for Deion's best interest.

"That's all I need to know."

Alex clasped his hands and stared at the ceiling for a moment, thinking that maybe it was a bad idea bringing the money to George. Maybe he should have just put it somewhere safe, only known to him and his mom. He quickly dismissed his concerns.

"Okay. Where's the money?" Alex presented George with two leather briefcases. He opened the first one and was glad to see that it was all hundred-dollar bills. When he closed the briefcase he asked, "There is no need to count this, is there?"

"You can count it, if you want, but it's all there."

George took another swig of water. The cash made him nervous. He planned to take it directly to one of his bank safe deposit boxes. The two men stood. Alex was a foot taller than George: he had flawless mahogany skin—a deep brown with a bit of a red tint, broad shoulders, very large hands, and a goatee. He was a man's man. With such a powerful physical appearance, Alex kept his style very low-key. His only display of wealth was a pricey diamond watch that his best friend and partner, Deion, had bought him for his birthday.

"I'll take good care of this, and you," his attorney said, extending his hand to Alex.

"With this type of money, I know you will," Alex stated without flinching. Alex gave one last lingering stare into his attorney's piercing eyes. "We do have a clear understanding…correct?"

"Of course. I've never let you down and I never will. That, I promise you." The men shook hands and Alex made his exit, with the same coolness as his entrance.

With Alex embarking on a new, potentially dangerous business venture, he wanted to make sure that he had all his bases covered. The higher up he seemed to go on the totem pole, the costlier his problems became, but Alex welcomed new challenges, because he had no intention of ever being a nickel and dime nigga again.

A KING PRODUCTION

Dior Comes Home...

Rich or Famous Part 2

JOY DEJA KING

AND CHRIS BOOKER

Prologue

Lorenzo stepped out of his black Bugatti Coupe and entered the non-descript building in East Harlem. Normally, Lorenzo would have at least one henchman with him, but he wanted complete anonymity. When he made his entrance, the man Lorenzo planned on hiring was patiently waiting.

"I hope you came prepared for what I need."

"I wouldn't have wasted my time if I hadn't," Lorenzo stated before pulling out two pictures from a manila envelope and tossing them on the table.

"This is her?"

"Yes, her name is Alexus. Study this face very carefully, 'cause this is the woman you're going to bring to me, so I can kill."

"Are you sure you don't want me to handle it? Murder is included in my fee."

"I know, but personally killing this backstabbing snake is a gift to myself"

"Who is the other woman?"

"Her name is Lala."

"Do you want her dead, too?"

"I haven't decided. For now, just find her whereabouts and any other pertinent information. She also has a young daughter. I want you to find out how the little girl is doing. That will determine whether Lala lives or dies."

"Is there anybody else on your hit list?"

"This is it for now, but that might change at any moment. Now, get on your job, because I want results ASAP," Lorenzo demanded before tossing stacks of money next to the photos.

"I don't think there's a need to count. I'm sure it's all there," the hit man said, picking up one of the stacks and flipping through the bills.

"No doubt, and you can make even more, depending on how quickly I see results."

"I appreciate the extra incentive."

"It's not for you, it's for me. Everyone that is responsible for me losing the love of my life will pay in blood. The sooner the better."

Lorenzo didn't say another word and instead made his exit. He came and delivered; the rest was up to the hit man he had hired. But Lorenzo wasn't worried, he was just one of the many killers on his payroll hired to do the exact same job. He wanted to guarantee that Alexus was delivered to him alive. In his heart, he not only blamed Alexus and Lala for getting him locked up, but also held both of them responsible for Dior taking her own life. As he sat in his jail cell, Lorenzo promised himself that once he got out, if need be he would spend the rest of his life making sure both women received the ultimate retribution.

A KING PRODUCTION

MAFIA

Princess

The Takeover

PART 5

A NOVEL

JOY DEJA KING

AND CHRIS BOOKER

Order Form

A King Production
P.O. Box 912
Collierville, TN 38027
www.joydejaking.com
www.twitter.com/joydejaking

Name: ______________________________
Address: ______________________________
City/State: ______________________________
Zip: ______________________________

QUANTITY	TITLES	PRICE	TOTAL
____	Bitch	$15.00	______
____	Bitch Reloaded	$15.00	______
____	The Bitch Is Back	$15.00	______
____	Queen Bitch	$15.00	______
____	Last Bitch Standing	$15.00	______
____	Superstar	$15.00	______
____	Ride Wit' Me	$12.00	______
____	Stackin' Paper	$15.00	______
____	Trife Life To Lavish	$15.00	______
____	Trife Life To Lavish II	$15.00	______
____	Stackin' Paper II	$15.00	______
____	Rich or Famous	$15.00	______
____	Rich or Famous Part 2	$15.00	______
____	Bitch A New Beginning	$15.00	______
____	Mafia Princess Part 1	$15.00	______
____	Mafia Princess Part 2	$15.00	______
____	Mafia Princess Part 3	$15.00	______
____	Mafia Princess Part 4	$15.00	______
____	Boss Bitch	$15.00	______
____	Baller Bitches Vol. 1	$15.00	______
____	Baller Bitches Vol. 2	$15.00	______
____	Bad Bitch	$15.00	______
____	Still The Baddest Bitch	$15.00	______
____	Princess Fever "Birthday Bash"	$9.99	______

Shipping/Handling (Via Priority Mail) $6.50 1-2 Books, $8.95 3-4 Books add $1.95 for ea. Additional book.

Total: $________ FORMS OF ACCEPTED PAYMENTS: Certified or government issued checks and money Orders, all mail in orders take 5-7 Business days to be delivered

Order Form

A King Production
P.O. Box 912
Collierville, TN 38027
www.joydejaking.com
www.twitter.com/joydejaking

Name: ____________________
Address: ____________________
City/State: ____________________
Zip: ____________________

QUANTITY	TITLES	PRICE	TOTAL
_____	Bitch	$15.00	_____
_____	Bitch Reloaded	$15.00	_____
_____	The Bitch Is Back	$15.00	_____
_____	Queen Bitch	$15.00	_____
_____	Last Bitch Standing	$15.00	_____
_____	Superstar	$15.00	_____
_____	Ride Wit' Me	$12.00	_____
_____	Stackin' Paper	$15.00	_____
_____	Trife Life To Lavish	$15.00	_____
_____	Trife Life To Lavish II	$15.00	_____
_____	Stackin' Paper II	$15.00	_____
_____	Rich or Famous	$15.00	_____
_____	Rich or Famous Part 2	$15.00	_____
_____	Bitch A New Beginning	$15.00	_____
_____	Mafia Princess Part 1	$15.00	_____
_____	Mafia Princess Part 2	$15.00	_____
_____	Mafia Princess Part 3	$15.00	_____
_____	Mafia Princess Part 4	$15.00	_____
_____	Boss Bitch	$15.00	_____
_____	Baller Bitches Vol. 1	$15.00	_____
_____	Baller Bitches Vol. 2	$15.00	_____
_____	Bad Bitch	$15.00	_____
_____	Still The Baddest Bitch	$15.00	_____
_____	Princess Fever "Birthday Bash"	$9.99	_____

Shipping/Handling (Via Priority Mail) $6.50 1-2 Books, $8.95 3-4 Books add $1.95 for ea. Additional book.

Total: $________**FORMS OF ACCEPTED PAYMENTS:** Certified or government issued checks and money Orders, all mail in orders take 5-7 Business days to be delivered